ABOUT THIS BOOK

Welcome to Havenwood Falls, home to sexy men, strong women, and neighbors who bite. Discover supernatural mystery, thrills, and romance in a place where everyone has a deep, dark, and often deadly secret. This is only but one . . .

Betrayed by love, Sherry Grimes flees the city, seeking solace in an unfamiliar place that calls to her from deep in the mountains. But her search for comfort goes awry when she's chased by a wolf through the forest, falls, and blacks out. She awakens in a strange room with a mysterious and forbidding—yet undeniably sexy—man by her side. So much for finding solitude. But despite the craziness that brings her to the small eccentric town, she discovers herself drawn into the magic that is Havenwood Falls.

Russell Higgins had long ago given up the idea of finding the one he could trust his secrets to—until he met Sherry. One look at the feisty woman with a broken heart has him defying his pack and rethinking his own ideas of his perfect mate. What he can't deny is the wolf inside, claiming the human as his.

Bradley Monahan wants Sherry back, and he would do anything to make that happen. Even fight the mysteries of a town that doesn't forgive transgressions.

While love may heal old wounds, it's the fresh ones that Sherry must overcome to find her way back home. Wherever that may be.

OLD WOUNDS

A HAVENWOOD FALLS NOVELLA

SUSAN BURDORF

HAVENWOOD FALLS BOOKS

Forget You Not by Kristie Cook

Old Wounds by Susan Burdorf

Fate, Love & Loyalty by E.J. Fechenda

The Winged & the Wicked by T.V. Hahn & Kristie Cook

Alpha's Queen by Lila Felix

Ink & Fire by R.K. Ryals

Lose You Not by Kristie Cook

Tragic Ink by Heather Hildenbrand

Nowhere to Hide by Belinda Boring

Flames Among the Frost by Amy Hale

Rock Me Gently by Susan Burdorf

From the Embers by Amy Miles

Defying Gravity by Kallie Ross

Break Me Not by Kristie Cook

How the Dead Lie by Stacey Rourke

The Lurkers Within by Danielle Bannister

The Collector: Awakening by Kristie Cook, R.K. Ryals, Belinda Boring & Nadirah Foxx

Addicted to You by Belinda Boring

Affliction Mine by C.J. Pinard

The Ward & the Wanderers by T.V. Hahn

Toil & Trouble by Melissa Wright

Of Salt and Stars by Seven Jane

Redefined by Morgan Wylie

Betrayal Among the Frost by Amy Hale

Forever Loyal by E.J. Fechenda

Fate's Demand by Emily Cyr

The Wu & the Wand by T.V. Hahn

A Demon's Redemption by JD Nelson

Also try the YA line, Havenwood Falls High; the historical paranormal line, Legends of Havenwood Falls; the darker, sexier side of town, Havenwood Falls Sin & Silk; and the local supernatural college, Sun & Moon Academy.

Stay up to date at www.HavenwoodFalls.com

BOOKS BY SUSAN BURDORF

I would like to dedicate this book to the readers who are about to discover the magic of Havenwood Falls.

CHAPTER 1

Sherry threw her Ford Focus into gear, wishing she was driving Brad's Viper instead of her old clunker. She ignored the vehicle's hesitation and the grinding sounds that came from underneath as she sped backwards out of the driveway without looking. Banging into the garbage can, she winced, knowing the heavy rubber container likely dented the side of the car, but not really caring.

She just needed to be gone, and to be gone as quickly as possible. As she spun the car to face the other end of the cul-de-sac, momentarily stopping to shift gears once more, Brad ran up and pounded on the window, startling her. He was bare-chested, his ripped muscles bulging with effort as he tried to force her to look at him. He wore a pair of gray sweatpants and little else. Normally the sight of his hard, athletic body would cause her to pause and stare at him with hunger, but today she only felt disgust and anger.

"Sherry, come on!" Brad's muted plea came through the closed window. Her fiancé—correction, *former* fiancé—raced barefoot alongside the slowly moving vehicle as she attempted to leave. He had one hand on the locked door handle and the other on the window as he tried to keep her from moving forward.

Sherry's heart beat out a rhythm that begged her to flatten him, but she waited for him to retreat back a step before she glared at him.

Rolling down the window, she said, "Get away from the car, or I'm gonna run over your toes."

Brad wisely stepped farther back, hands raised in surrender. His face turned a bright shade of red. He tossed his black hair out of his eyes. Pointing a finger at her, he said, "Go ahead, run off like a baby. You never were a good lay. I don't need you anyway."

"You will when the rent comes due next week," Sherry spat out before she sped off down the street. In the rearview mirror, which Sherry mentally kicked herself for looking into, she saw the blonde draped around him, rubbing his chest and consoling him in the only way a strumpet like her knew how to.

The girl was dressed in the silk robe Brad had given Sherry on her last birthday. Her favorite silk robe. The one Brad said brought out the blue in her eyes and the sexy in her toned and petite body. She was half-tempted to whip the car around and rip the silk off the woman's slender, tanned form, but decided to forgo that pleasure in favor of getting the heck away from there. Flipping her dark hair over her shoulders, she forced herself to keep her eyes on the road.

A short while later, blinded by tears, she nearly sideswiped a delivery truck and city bus before her pounding heart calmed down and she could breathe normally again. After several hours, with the radio blasting rock music loud enough to melt her eardrums, Sherry pulled over to the side of the road into a small rest area. She had no idea where she was, or where she was going, but something had told her to keep driving, so she followed her gut instinct.

The brisk spring air, chilled with the promise of more winter this close to the mountains of Colorado, greeted her as she emerged from the car. Stepping into a slushy puddle, she groaned in frustration. These were her favorite black heels, their leather now ruined forever in the salty, half-melted snow that encased her foot up to the ankle.

Sherry grabbed her cloak from the passenger side and wrapped the thin material around her cream-colored silk blouse. Neither article of clothing was any protection from the cold air that whipped around her. Her dark hair had fallen from the loose bun she'd put it in earlier while driving to keep it out of her eyes. She shivered.

The sound of laughter drew her eyes to a family walking toward the entrance to the building that housed the bathrooms and snack machines. The little girl held tightly to her father's hand, while the boy —in his mother's arms as he was just a toddler—hugged the woman tightly. Looking over her shoulder at her husband who walked slightly behind them, the woman smiled at something he'd said with a look of complete adoration, which he returned with an easy smile of his own. Sherry felt her throat tighten in jealousy.

Would she ever see anyone look at her like that?

She'd thought Brad would be that one, the one who would make her heart sing with passion that could last forever, but he obviously played their love song out of tune. What was so wrong with her that she couldn't find anyone to love her for longer than it took to cash her paycheck?

She'd met Brad in church, for Christ's sake. How could he have turned out to be such a snake? Was this bimbo the first, as he'd claimed while throwing on his pants to chase after her when she fled? Or was this one just the first he'd been caught with? If she hadn't come home from work early today due to a gas leak near the therapy office at the middle school, she never would have known anything about what he was up to when she was gone each day. Who knew how long this had been going on without her knowledge? Brad certainly wasn't going to tell her, and the bimbo was barely able to string a sentence together, so no help there.

Shivering in the cold, Sherry already regretted her hasty decision to run away. She should have made him, and the bimbo, of course, leave. She considered turning around and driving home, but the last thing she wanted to do was have another argument with him or, worse yet, admit she was wrong to leave so quickly. Even though she knew she wasn't.

That love nest of his was *her* apartment, dammit. She should have made *him* leave. Her face darkened as she remembered the sounds that greeted her when she'd opened the door, sounds she was all too familiar with making herself after a few glasses of good wine and great jazz.

Pinching her lips, she closed her eyes, willing the tears not to fall.

"Lady?" said a small voice to her right. "Are you okay? Do you need a sucker?"

Slowly opening her eyes, Sherry said, "No, thank you." Under her breath she muttered, "I *am* the sucker," which came out louder than she intended.

Sherry looked down to see a tiny blonde girl holding up a bright red sucker, the kind the dentist used to give her back when she was young, if she was a good girl and didn't squirm too much in the seat while they drilled her teeth. She'd always thought it ironic that a dentist would give sugar on a stick to a kid whose teeth he'd just worked on, but she hadn't complained too loudly. And it *had* seemed to ease the pain, at least for a little while.

"Thank you," Sherry said, reconsidering. She took the sucker the little girl offered and smiled, hoping her mouth made the appropriate shape and wouldn't scare the child. Sherry wasn't sure what to do next, as the girl didn't seem to want to leave.

"I am so sorry. I hope Destiny wasn't bothering you too much." The little girl's mother took her daughter by the hand and gently tugged her away.

Sherry smiled crookedly. "Destiny? Perfect name for the first person I speak to right after the disaster of my current life. Almost like a sign."

A sign? Of course it was a sign. Sherry was a firm believer that if you stood still long enough, the universe would find a way to connect with you. Watching the tiny girl and her mother walk with hands clasped tightly, she wasn't surprised when the girl turned, locked eyes with her, and gave Sherry a solemn wink before getting in the car with her family and driving off.

Sherry entered, then stood in the middle of the information building as she looked around. She was surrounded by maps marking the nearest hiking trails, along with brochures advertising tourist traps, which were neatly lined up on the wall in metal racks. The slick, curved, white walls and cheap marble flooring somehow both soothed and unsettled her. Sherry felt the walls closing in on her, although nothing was moving. She felt something happening—changing—inside her. She breathed deeply, eyes closed, and waited to see if the universe had another sign for her.

But nothing came. At least not right away.

No one said, "Go home, patch things up with your skanky boyfriend, and forget that he tends to like other women once in a while." Conversely, nothing else said, "Forget that jerk, keep driving."

Then she heard the soft *swish-swish* of leather-soled shoes on the floor.

"Can I help you, miss?" A kind dark-skinned man, with eyes like chips of coal in his lined and weathered face, looked at her in concern. "Are you lost?" He wore a dark green uniform with a slim silver badge that announced him as BRAD.

Sherry wanted to laugh out loud at the irony of meeting someone with her ex-boyfriend's name, but swallowed back the mirthless sound instead. Sometimes the universe could be cruel. She shook her head, but her watery eyes gave away her true emotional state. The man patted her arm and then squeezed it as he led her over to where the brightly colored and labeled maps rested.

"Perhaps you're looking for a nice place to visit?"

Sherry felt herself gently propelled closer toward the maps. She took the one he proffered to her, barely glancing at it. The second she touched it, she felt a tingle, gentle and insistent, travel up her arm. Nothing uncomfortable or painful—it was more like the pins-and-needles feeling when her arm fell asleep after resting her head on it for a while.

"This is a brochure for a lovely town not far from here called Havenwood Falls. A lot of folks find the town quite pleasant to visit, and I'm sure you will, too."

Sherry raised an eyebrow as she looked at the one-page, double-sided flyer he'd handed to her. The old man stood in front of her, slightly stooped and expectant, as if her decision mattered a great deal to him.

Sherry's eye was caught by the promise of a "cabin in paradise," and she was sold before she even knew what else to say.

Chuckling as if he knew the answer before he asked, the old man said, "You have a plan now?"

"Why, yes," Sherry said, answering his twinkling eyes with a shy smile of her own. "I think I do. These cabins sound wonderful. I see a number down here. I'm going to call and see if they have anything available."

"Good idea. You'd better move on now. There's a storm heading this way soon, and it wouldn't do to get caught in it. Those late spring squalls can be quite temperamental in the mountains. Oh, and miss," the old man said as she started to turn away, "the town is a bit difficult to find. You can take the shuttle outside, or if you prefer to drive your own vehicle, you are welcome to follow the bus for the best way to get there. I strongly urge you to do that. The shuttle bus will be leaving in about ten minutes, though, so you'd better hurry."

Sherry looked where he pointed and saw a large bus idling in the section reserved for buses and trucks to park. She couldn't see through the tinted windows, so wasn't sure if it was full already or not. Since there was so little time to get on the bus if she wanted to take it, and since she was planning to rent a cabin and would need her car, she decided not to take the bus. But she would definitely follow it. She had a feeling the old man was not lying about it being a difficult town to find and wondered why. Mountain roads could be tricky sometimes, with quick turns, and perhaps that was the reason why. Either way, she was getting excited at the thought of having a plan.

Sherry nodded. Chuckling once she walked outside, she grinned at the kindness of the old man. He'd been pushy, but pretty darn cute in spite of it. She liked him. Looking back through the glass doors, she was surprised not to see him standing in the doorway watching her. Instead, she could make out a tall, stocky woman behind the desk, shuffling papers and talking to an elderly couple who had just walked up.

After calling the number on the flyer, Sherry was relieved to find there was one cabin left. Because it was higher up on the mountain than she would have liked, she hesitated before committing to the idea of the cabin. *I'm just planning to hike the area for a few days until things have a little time to cool off at home,* she reasoned, justifying both the expense and the remoteness of the cabin.

"That will be three hundred dollars for the week," the woman on the other end of the line said.

Sherry gasped in surprise. "Are you sure? That seems pretty cheap."

"Oh, yes, ma'am. Your cabin is very rustic, therefore a little cheaper," the woman replied. Her voice sounded pleasant and certain, exactly the way a customer service person should sound.

Sherry gave the woman her card number and then, just as the woman hung up, thought of a question she needed to ask. When she tried to call back, the number was busy. Hanging up, Sherry decided to go back inside and thank the old man for his help and try the number later.

Inside, Sherry waited a minute until the woman behind the counter was free. Sheila's name badge was slightly crooked and not as shiny, but still lettered the same. When Sheila looked up, Sherry smiled sweetly and said, "I wonder if you might give that sweet old guy, Brad, a message for me?"

"Brad?" Sheila's expression was puzzled and annoyed, like she had plenty of better things to do than play secretary.

"Yes, the nice man who helped me a few minutes ago."

"How did he help you?" the woman asked. Her expression had changed from annoyed to cautious, as if afraid of what Sherry might answer.

"Well, he gave me this flyer, the one about Havenwood Falls and renting a cabin. Let him know that's what I've decided to do. And I owe it all to him. So please, tell him thank you."

Sheila hesitated. Biting her lip, she folded her hands together on the desk and stared Sherry squarely in the face. "I'm not sure what game you are playing at here, young lady, but we have no one working here named Brad. And I have never heard of Havenwood Falls. What are you trying to pull?"

Sherry, totally shocked by the woman's attitude—which she felt was totally uncalled for and very hostile—stepped away from the desk. Holding the flyer in front of her, she spoke slowly as if making sure the woman behind the desk would understand the words she was saying. "I just met one of your employees, a nice old man named Brad—it said so on his badge—and he recommended I check into a cabin listed on this flyer."

Sherry flashed the flyer in front of the other woman's face for emphasis and was shocked to discover it did not say "Havenwood Falls" in bold black lettering, but instead encouraged visitors to visit a ghost town about forty miles down the road in the opposite direction.

"*What?*" Sherry dropped the flyer on the desk as if it burned her hand, her face bright pink, and slowly backed away as a young man wearing a backpack walked up to the desk for assistance.

Sherry practically ran from the building and jumped in the car, not surprised to see her hands shaking. *What is going on? I know I had the flyer for Havenwood Falls in my hand. How else could I have called that place for a cabin? Now how will I ever find my way there?*

Sherry looked over at the passenger side of the car, and her eyes widened in shock. On the seat next to her lay the flyer she was sure she'd just dropped on the counter in front of Sheila. And there, written in bold black print, were the words, "HAVENWOOD FALLS. DISCOVER THE MAGIC."

What an odd town motto, she thought as she set the GPS for the location of the cabin rental office where the woman had said they would leave her a key.

"Strange," she said aloud as she tapped the GPS. "What is wrong with this thing? Why won't it pull up the address?"

Sherry shook the device, but nothing changed. She turned it off, and then on again, and still nothing changed. The address was not pulling up at all.

"Now what?" Sherry slumped back in the seat, trying not to cry. This was just too much.

Ahead of her she saw the large bus pulling away from its parking spot. On the side of the bus were the words Havenwood Falls in large lettering with picturesque scenes of the mountains. Without thinking about it too much, Sherry decided she would follow the bus like the old man suggested. It looked like the kind of bus one might charter or the kind tourists use.

Putting the car in gear, once again ignoring the grinding sound, she backed slowly out of her parking spot and pointed the nose of the car toward the highway. Something weird was going on, and she felt like she was in an episode of *The Twilight Zone*, one of her favorite shows. The grainy black-and-white program had been a staple in her household, much preferred over the banal sitcoms that passed for quality television these days.

As she drove, her phone buzzed, a bright blue-white light signaling an incoming call. She'd turned the ringer off earlier to avoid Brad's many attempts to contact her, so she heard nothing but the buzzing.

Humming to a song on the radio as she ignored the phone, she focused on the road ahead of her. Keeping the bus in sight was pretty easy, since it was so large. She felt the excitement building at the prospect of spending time alone. This was the start of a great adventure. There was no doubt of that in her mind.

Sherry hoped there was a town along the way with a store where she could purchase some clothing appropriate for an extended stay in a cabin, or that Havenwood Falls would be able to supply her with what she needed. She was certain her hastily packed suitcase had nothing she could wear in the woods, and she would need to purchase some food, too. The rumbling of her stomach was a reminder she hadn't eaten in several hours, and the trauma of her situation was starting to take its toll on her. She was starving.

As she drove, she caught sight of a sign on the side of the road noting that Havenwood Falls was just six miles down the road. Not understanding why, she felt almost giddy at the prospect of spending time in the mountains near what she was sure would be a quaint tourist town, if the flyer was a truthful representation of its appearance, that is. After nearly six hours on the road, she was ready to stop for the night.

She didn't realize how far this place was from Albuquerque until she glanced at her phone. But she didn't regret one minute of the drive. It had been beautiful driving through the mountains. She hadn't been this spontaneous in years, and it felt good to be free. She hadn't noticed until now how being with Brad had held her back from doing things she enjoyed. He hated the woods, bugs were not his friends, and he swelled up like a dirigible anytime he got bit by something as inconsequential as a mosquito.

She chuckled as she remembered his reaction the one time she'd suggested going weekend camping. He'd just about fainted at the thought of his model-perfect body deformed by nature, a place he referred to as "Alcatraz with trees," since he felt imprisoned if not near civilization, otherwise known as his local craft-beer brewery.

"The only nature I ever want to be in, baby," he'd said in perfect seriousness, "is the kind where they have an infinity pool and girls in skimpy white outfits bringing you those drinks with umbrellas in them."

She'd thought he was adorable then. She knew the truth now.

But she'd gone along with it, feeling that being in love meant making sacrifices so the other would feel appreciated. Now she wondered what he'd ever given up for her. She couldn't think of a single thing he'd sacrificed for her good. It had always been her doing the compromising.

She pinched her lips tightly as she thanked her lucky stars they hadn't married yet. It was bad enough imagining the untangling they would have to do when it came time for him to leave now. A marriage would have meant a split of everything right down the middle, and she had a lot of memories tied up in the things in her apartment, not something she was willing to share with someone who treated her so badly. There were photo albums and valuable pieces of decorative art and small treasures that had belonged to her now-deceased parents. Most of the items had been in her family for a long time, and she was not willing to let him take anything just because he'd warmed her bed for a while.

Sherry attempted the phone number once more and sighed in frustration when there was no answer. She paused a moment, considering her options. Should she go forward, or back? Thinking of Brad, his expression smug and sure of himself if she went back, she pinched her lips and decided back was not a place on her GPS. She would only be able to go forward. So Havenwood Falls it would be. She hoped the old man was right, that she would find in Havenwood Falls the answer to her prayers.

"Yep," she said softly. "This might turn out to be the stupidest idea I have ever had, but—" She paused as the bus increased the distance between them and she stepped on the accelerator to keep it in sight. "Havenwood Falls sounds like exactly what I need right now."

CHAPTER 2

*R*ussell—"Rusty" to his friends—Higgins looked out over the forest and sniffed. The wind brought the smell of something unexpected. Rain? Or something else? He could smell the coming storm. It was still a little while away, but it was definitely going to bring some kind of moisture.

Shaking his shoulders free of his shirt, he shivered in the sudden cold air that struck his bare skin. His muscles contracted across his ripped chest as he stretched his arms toward the sky. It was nearly time for him to take his wolf form and roam the woods on his nightly patrol.

He folded his shirt, shaking it free of leaves from where he'd been laying on the ground just moments before. His thoughts were jumbled, not just by the feelings of unease that permeated his mind, but by a conversation he'd had earlier that day with his distant cousin, Sheriff Kasun.

Rusty hated being boxed into a corner, and his cousin had just given Rusty an ultimatum he wasn't willing to accept. He liked the freedom of being in the forest, with no demands greater than those necessary for survival in the woods. The needs and wants of the human world exhausted him. If he had a choice, he would never leave his beloved woods. But that might not be an option for him much longer.

While Rusty prepared himself for the change, he replayed the brief conversation he'd had with his cousin in the store that morning.

"Choices," the sheriff had said, "aren't always of our choosing. Sometimes the choices are made for us. You know we would like you to return to the pack. I wish you would think about it. The choice is yours, of course, but we would welcome you back."

The memory of that conversation resurfaced as he watched the sun give way to the night in a sky flushed pink and gold, chased by the deeper blue of gathering dusk.

"Curse you, cousin," Rusty said softly to the night air. "I like my life just the way it is." And he did. He was happy being alone.

Like a petulant boy, told he couldn't have that extra cookie, Rusty stuck out his chin in defiance. Why did he have to disturb his way of life? Why did he have to make a choice? All he wanted to do was roam his beloved woods, keep to himself in his cabin, and not interact with the people of the town unless he had to. That was how it had been for too many years to count, so why did he have to change his life?

Havenwood Falls had existed on the edge of discovery for generations too numerous for him to count. He didn't like the idea of having to join the Kasun pack again. Just because he was a wolf-shifter didn't mean he had to be in a pack, at least not in his mind. Rusty understood how some might like that feeling of camaraderie and unity that a pack brought to a group of the supernaturals, but he had always been a loner, and he wasn't about to change that, no matter what his cousin wanted.

His woods, his trees, and the animals that occupied the environs of the kingdom he protected were all he needed to survive. He was most content here, on this land. Something about these woods calmed him, soothed his soul, and he wasn't willing to give it up for a house in town complete with the wife and 2.2 children the rest of the pack seemed to find satisfying.

For him, the confines of four walls would be like a prison, no matter the pretty trappings. His forest was the only home he needed. His cabin was sparse, barely furnished with only the pieces he'd made from the offerings the forest gave him. His own two hands had constructed the cabin years before. He had a generator to run the electricity that powered the lights. Although he preferred the romance of firelight for the most part, he conceded that a good electric lamp was a blessing when reading after dark.

His cabin was a tight little building with a sleeping loft above the main floor, and wide beams in a dark wood lined the ceiling. His bedroom was on the ground floor, with a rough bathroom just off it. The kitchen, which held a refrigerator and a table with two chairs, was cozy. He rarely used the second chair, though, as he discouraged visitors. There were no pictures on the walls, and no curtains were necessary on the windows, as his cabin was secluded in the woods.

He was not an ugly man, his body kept fit by his nightly patrols in the forest, his hair a rusty brownish-red that gave him his nickname, which was also a variation of his given name. His eyes, a deep chocolate brown, seemed to appeal to the women he sought for comfort, none of whom had ever been to his home. He preferred to meet them away from his cabin.

So far, none had roused his mating desire, merely his body's need for momentary comfort. He wasn't a cruel man, though. He always let the women know it was not their attractions, or lack thereof, that couldn't hold him, but rather his need to roam was too strong. He never gave out false hope. While a woman might turn his attentions down based on those terms, there was always someone else willing to take her place.

Sometimes he worried he was too careful, that he would have no one to pass on his legacy to, but when those doubts crept in, Rusty usually brushed them aside, knowing in his heart that the right woman would come along. He had decided a long time ago he would not settle for less than his perfect mate.

"Time to go," he whispered to himself, surprised at how he was suddenly so melancholy. What had set off this strange mood? He quickly took off the rest of his clothes, sliding pants down strong lean thighs, already furring with his signature rusty color. His boots had already been kicked off, his socks placed neatly inside the boots.

He slipped off his remaining clothes and stood naked in the

waning light of the sun. He stretched to his full height, straightening his spine, reveling in the feel of the night's chill wind on his bare skin.

That brief moment before he became the wolf was fraught with so many questions. Would it hurt this time? Would he survive the night and return to his human form with the sunrise, or would he forget the rules and end up a wolf forever? He had only once come close to remaining in wolf form, and it was not an experience he wanted to repeat. The way his mind had gone from human to wolf and refused to return to his intelligent thinking had been a fluke—at least he'd thought so at the time. But now, with many changes gone past that nearly tragic day, he'd come to understand the true consequence of allowing the wolf full control of his mind and body, and he knew he'd never allow it to happen again.

The tingling that signaled the beginning of the change intensified, and he turned toward the distant horizon to watch where the sun sank lower in the sky as it slipped away from view.

Where the setting sun touched his body, he glowed with a highlight of red that set fire to his skin. He closed his eyes, face raised upward to welcome the moon, his mistress. What need had he of a woman, when he could be anything he wanted by the silvery light of the white orb that welcomed his change with such hunger each night?

Bending down, he stuffed his clothes and boots into the backpack that lay next to them. He quickly placed the backpack in his hiding place. When he changed back into his human form, he would need those clothes once more. The discomfort that signaled the change was growing stronger, and he knew his time in this human form was growing shorter. It wouldn't do to begin the transformation without taking care of his clothes first. He'd forgotten once to do that, and the end result had been a walk home without any, not something he wanted to make a practice of, not that anyone saw him this deep in the woods. Still, one never knew who might be hiking or wandering the woods these days. He breathed a sigh of relief when all was ready.

In moments, he felt the familiar stirrings of his body's shift. The pain had long ago become something less than euphoric, but he still shivered with the anticipation of what would come next.

He crouched down as his body began the transformation into its supernatural wolf form. His teeth elongated and his limbs shortened and thickened, their muscles popping and snapping as they reshaped.

He howled, unable to stop the primal reaction to his new form, and shook his fur into place. Lifting his head, he looked around and howled at the moon once more. It was a long, extended howl, one meant to announce his arrival to both the forest and himself. He liked giving fair warning.

His mouth curved into a fierce smile, one that might frighten children, although he was a gentle wolf, not like some of his brethren who liked to rip out the throats of their victims. He rarely fed while in this shape, though the restraint took all his willpower. His teacher, the one who'd long ago taught him about being a wolf shape, had warned him that if you forgot your humanity and became the beast, you could never go back. Human blood was the surest way to cross that line. No matter how angry he became, he never allowed himself to reach the point of no return. There had been times over the years when his willpower had been tested by poachers, or butchers as he liked to refer to them, who thought the forest was their supermarket. He'd met some such hunters not long ago, but since that encounter, they'd pretty much stayed away from his forest.

He'd heard rumors when he was in town of a couple guys in the bar talking about doing the town a favor by ridding them of "that beast," but they'd been convinced by Sheriff Kasun to leave the woods alone and to stay away if they knew what was good for them.

That was what had brought his cousin out to see him in the first place, but the battle to bring Rusty into the pack had been an ongoing one for quite a while. While the alpha's attempts to coerce Rusty into the fold were half-hearted, his reasons were not. Rusty was aware of the difficulties facing the supernaturals as the human world crept closer to their secrets, but he wasn't yet ready to give up his freedom. This forest was his home—end of story. Warnings about the humans and to be wary of them had been part of his life for a long time. Not encroaching on their world too much was a constant dance of vigilance he was willing to choreograph as long as it meant he could remain free to go where he pleased. So eating a human, even ones who deserved it, was not on his to-do list.

Fear of that permanent change, and how it would keep his human side from being in greater control, was something he kept in his mind always. He might feed if a small animal happened to cross his path while he was running, but most in the forest now knew him and stayed in their homes until he'd passed by. He ignored them, and they had all learned to exist together.

As his mind slowly became the mind of the wolf, his alter ego's intelligence almost as great as Rusty's, the man stretched his wolf legs and began his nightly prowl.

Sniffing the air, he caught whiff of an unfamiliar scent and turned his nose in that direction. His super-sensitive ears caught the sound of a car, and fearing it might be more poachers, he headed in that direction, his pads making soft footfalls on the forest floor as he hurried toward the road.

CHAPTER 3

A short distance later, Sherry's confidence was shattered when her car began making a very distinct sound of distress. As it rattled to a stop, a small puff of steam rising from beneath the hood, she cursed. Why, oh why, hadn't she taken Brad's car instead? At least his was kept in tip-top shape so he would have transportation to his auditions. In her haste to leave, she'd grabbed the first set of keys she could find and that had been hers, even though she knew her car was in need of a trip to the garage.

Sherry leaned forward until she bumped her head on the steering wheel and tried not to cry. *Not now*, she thought, biting her lip to control her frustration. She turned the key, hoping the car was just being its usual temperamental self, but not surprised when the loud click proved her worst fears had come true. The car was momentarily toast.

"Great, just great," she said, trying to remain calm. The sky was full dark now, adding to her unease at being alone. The road was bordered on both sides by thick forest, and she hadn't passed, or been passed by, a single vehicle since losing sight of the Havenwood Falls bus.

Reaching for her cell phone, she groaned when she saw there was no reception here. She couldn't even call for a tow or a ride. She didn't think they would have Uber out here in the sticks, but she'd never know since she couldn't use her phone. In this age of technology crowding into every corner of the world, how could this place not have reception? Perhaps the mountains were disrupting the signal because not even a single bar was lit.

"That figures," she said bitterly, tears threatening to fall. She sniffed. Closing her eyes, she leaned back in her seat. *Now what? I suppose I can walk to the town. It's only around six miles. I used to do that in the city all the time. But at least in the city I had sidewalks, interesting things to look at on the way, and it's a concrete jungle, not a forest with wild animals or worse waiting to jump out at me.*

She breathed in and out slowly a few times, gathering her thoughts and considering her options. Since the traffic was nonexistent, there was no rescue coming from the direction of the rest area. Maybe if she walked a bit farther down the road, the forest would thin out, and she could find a place to make a call. That would have to do. She felt better already, having a plan in mind.

Then she remembered the flimsy shoes she had on, and she groaned again. She would never be able to walk half a mile in those shoes, let alone six if she had to walk the whole distance to town. She thought back to what she'd packed and shook her head at her foolishness. She hadn't packed any extra shoes at all, not even a pair of flip flops. She'd been in such a hurry, she didn't remember even packing extra underwear.

"Stupid, stupid," she cursed out loud.

After a couple minutes of swearing at herself, she took a deep breath. Trying the key in the ignition one last time, she wasn't surprised when it didn't work, but she hit the steering wheel anyway, ignoring the sting of pain.

Darkness had now completely taken over, the last rays of sunlight disappearing behind the mountain peaks. She shivered in the chilly air. If she stayed where she was, waiting for a car that may or may not pass, she might freeze to death. Best to start moving and do it soon.

Opening her car door, she stepped out and shivered again as a blast of cold air struck her through the thin blouse. She walked to the back of the car and opened the trunk.

Reaching in, she pulled the suitcase to her and nearly jumped for joy when she found a sweatshirt, which she immediately threw on over her blouse. The only thing that would have made her happier would have been to discover a better pair of shoes for walking, but unfortunately, she didn't find a single pair.

She debated taking the suitcase with her, but decided it would be too hard to walk and drag the case behind her even though it had wheels. Surely the town would have a store where she could purchase clothes and shoes? And she'd be back with the tow truck soon, so stay it would.

Decision made, she zipped the case back up and closed the trunk. Slapping her hands together, she was surprised at how the sound comforted her. She hadn't realized until just now how alone she was out here on this road. She listened to the sounds of the night around her. From the trees on either side, she heard creatures stirring in the underbrush. She shivered, wondering what creatures were going about their night hunts.

In the distance, an owl hooted softly, followed by the sound of wings as the bird took flight. At least, she hoped it was the owl. She shook her head and grinned wryly at her overactive imagination. Honestly, what did she expect to find in the woods—a ghost, or vampires, or werewolves? She cursed those late night horror flicks she'd watched as a child for giving her the idea that creatures lurked around every corner or behind every tree.

Overhead, the stars that dotted the night sky gave off a faint light. The moon, what she called a fingernail moon, was still low enough in the sky that its sliver of silver gave off little more than a glow, but clouds were gathering overhead, and she wasn't sure how much longer she would have that limited light.

Sherry opened the door to the passenger side, grabbed her purse, and pulled it over her shoulder. She then opened the glove box and rifled through the papers and other items until she finally found the flashlight she knew was there. She found a pack of cigarettes and a lighter shoved in the back of the glove box and frowned. Brad must have hidden them in there, although he'd told her he quit. Just one more lie to tally against him. How stupid of him to hide them in her car. While this was a small transgression on his part compared to what had driven her to this deserted stretch of road, it was still a mark in the glad-I-am-not-with-him-anymore column.

She pulled the flashlight out, but threw the cigarettes back inside. Turning on the flashlight, she sighed in relief when its silver beam shot out. She'd been half afraid, the way her luck was running tonight, that the batteries would be dead. On this darkened road, with who knew what kinds of creatures lurking about, she didn't want to have to walk by starlight alone.

"Okay, girl," she spoke into the night air in an effort to keep herself from being afraid, "no time like the present to get moving."

Straightening her shoulders and shining the light in front of her, Sherry started walking, hoping the next six miles would pass quickly. Keeping her eyes on the road, she ignored the feeling of night creatures watching her. Her heels, totally inappropriate for walking, clicked loudly on the asphalt. She hunched her shoulders inside her sweatshirt and quickened her pace, trying to keep herself warm. The night air had dropped at least ten degrees since she'd left the warmth of the vehicle, and she knew it was only going to grow colder as the clouds gathered in the sky, intermittently blocking the moon and stars.

As she walked, she tried to think what she would do once she reached the cabin. *If* she made it, she corrected herself. If her luck didn't turn, who knew if she would make it to the refuge of the cabin before the next day? Hopefully the car was reparable, and she could be on her way quickly.

She focused on the walk, ignoring the rustling of the leaves and sigh of wind through the trees, and the sounds of soft padded footsteps.

Wait. Footsteps?

She whirled around, flashlight beam pointed behind and around her in a wild arc as she tried to identify the source of the sounds she'd heard. There. She pointed the flashlight in the direction of the sound and thought she caught the flash of something red in the beam.

But the closer she walked toward the shoulder of the road that rimmed the edge of the forest, the more she thought she was just being ridiculous.

"Come on, girl," she chided herself as she walked slowly forward, toward the thick brush and tree line at the shoulder's graveled edge, "don't make trouble for yourself. There's nothing there. Even if there were, it was probably just a raccoon or something like that. There couldn't possibly be anything more dangerous out here. Oh Lord," she whispered as she turned back toward the road, "if you get me out of this alive, I promise to stop making fun of those church shows on TV."

The only answer to her prayer was a gust that chilled her to the bones. Was that agreement? Or just the cold night air reminding her she was alone on a dark and nearly deserted road? She narrowed her eyes as her flashlight caught the glint of something silver in the brush lining the road. She pointed the beam where she'd seen the flash of silver but saw nothing. Shivering, she tugged the sweatshirt tighter around her body as she backed away from the edge of the road.

She straightened her shoulders, turned herself in the direction the sign had indicated for Havenwood Falls, and walked into the fog that now covered the road in front of her.

CHAPTER 4

*R*usty watched her go, a strange tingling singing in his blood. She wasn't remarkably beautiful, but in the sudden patch of moonlight that had fallen on her before she turned away from where he was hiding, she'd looked ethereal. Haunting. Ghostly, almost. A woman, he knew immediately, with steel in her blood.

A woman he wanted to know more about.

He followed her, carefully picking his way among the underbrush as he kept hidden while paralleling her path. There was something about her that drew him. Obviously, she was human—he scented only her light flowery perfume. Jasmine, he thought. There wasn't a hint of anything supernatural about her, and yet . . . and yet there was something drawing him to her and her to the town.

He had thought for just a moment that she'd spotted him. The way she'd walked toward the forest's edge as if she sought something, perhaps him, had him holding his breath until she hesitated and moved back and then down the road.

Her car must have been the one he'd heard earlier. He watched as she headed toward town. If she intended to walk the six miles, he would have to follow her the whole way. There were creatures in the woods tonight, creatures that she shouldn't come across. Her disappearance might be hard to explain.

He padded softly ahead of her, making sure nothing crossed her path. Most of the forest creatures, sensing his presence, had already gone to ground, but it wasn't the usual beasts he worried about. It was the unusual. The kind the town might have a hard time explaining if something happened to her.

He sent out a silent prayer that no one but him would be out tonight. He hadn't sensed anyone, but one never knew who might decide this was a good time to go out and about in the woods on their way to a feeding or other assignation. Sometimes the high school shifter kids were brought out here for lessons on their crafts and legacies. He hadn't seen any of the witches, vampires, other shifters, or their children out in these particular woods in quite a while, but that meant nothing.

So lost in thought was he that he missed when the woman he followed stopped in the road. She was adjusting a shoe that seemed to have come loose. He grinned, noting that her shoes were definitely not the kind for a long walk, and wondered why she hadn't changed them when she'd put on her sweatshirt.

Watching the moon's faint light as it disappeared behind the gathering clouds, Rusty silently cursed. Lifting his nose, he whimpered slightly at the change in the smell of the wind. The storm was not far off now.

This woman had better hurry, or she would be on the road when the bad weather hit. The wind smelled of cold air and bitter snow. This was not going to be a quick storm. He had a feeling it would hit hard when it came.

He watched the woman shiver. Maybe she felt the storm coming, too? She looked up, and a few seconds later, she began walking again, this time a little quicker.

Without realizing he was doing it, he quickened his steps to keep close to her and stepped on a branch. The crack of the broken twig reverberated through the woods like a gunshot, and the woman whirled around, the flashlight's beam brushing over the top of the bush under which he had taken shelter.

He narrowed his eyes until they were nearly closed to keep their gleam from lighting when the flashlight crossed over and around the bush. The woman did not move any closer, but he could tell she was nervous by the way she kept jabbing the beam of light here and there in a scattershot attempt to see if anything was there.

He crouched down, barely breathing, opening his eyes just a slit to see when she moved on. As she moved away, her scent grew fainter, and he found himself making his movements match hers.

After a few moments of pacing closer and then away from the forest's edge, the woman began walking toward town again, this time faster than before. He cursed himself for his carelessness. The last thing he wanted to do was alarm her.

He sped up to keep pace with her, bounding over fallen logs and landing soft-footed on the path. This went on for at least a mile before the woman slowed. Her exhaustion was showing. He wished he could change back, reassure her she was doing the right thing by heading into town, but if she was afraid of an invisible creature in the dark, he was certain his naked form would scare her even more. He had no clothes hidden in this part of the woods.

No, he would have to continue to watch her in his wolf form, at least until he could change to more suitable attire than his birthday suit to greet her in his human form.

He observed her as she walked. She was cautious, glancing left and right as she kept up a pace that might have exhausted others, but seemed to keep her invigorated. He grinned in spite of himself. She was feisty; he would give her that.

It was obvious she was afraid, but she wasn't giving in to it. Other women in her situation might have cried or carried on, or made comments about their plight, but she never uttered a word. She kept moving at a pace that would require a predator to reveal themselves, in shoes that were most likely uncomfortable in the office, and on this surface, must be killing her.

He chuckled, which in his wolf form came out more as a thin growl, as she stopped to check her shoe. She jerked her head up when a long thin howl caused her to freeze.

Drat! Rusty thought, whipping his head around. *Who is out here in the woods playing games?* He didn't recognize the howl or the one that answered it. His first duty was to the forest, but he knew, looking over at the woman who was frozen in place, that he couldn't abandon her, either.

Had someone seen her? Was someone going to cause her harm? Not in his woods. But where had that sound come from? He raised his head above the underbrush, instinct to protect the forest overcoming his need for secrecy, and sniffed. He moved onto the road to get a clear view of the forest and down the highway, forgetting momentarily that she was also in the road and now had a clear view of him.

Nothing. He couldn't smell a thing out of the ordinary. The rich loam of the forest filled his nostrils, mixed with vegetation, the faint odors of animals, and the woman's strong flowery scent.

The scream from behind shocked him.

He whirled around, his teeth bared, ready for battle to defend his property, when the beam of light struck him in the face. The woman screamed again and threw the flashlight in his direction, hitting him on the edge of his nose.

He howled in pain. The most sensitive part of his body was his nose after all, and her aim had been perfect. He howled again, and she screamed, then ran for the edge of the forest and disappeared into the thick brush.

He heard her screaming as she crashed through the vegetation at a speed not safe for the darkness of the night, and he cursed silently.

By the Moon! He howled. *Instead of running into the woods, why didn't she keep running down the road? And why did she throw her flashlight instead of keeping it? Foolish, foolish, foolish.*

Even as he thought it, he was giving chase. Just as he rounded a large boulder, he found her on the faint path made by deer crossing the valley. The trail was barely more than a thin ribbon of dirt bordering the side of a hill, but the human girl stood in it, pointing a large stick at him. On one side of her was a rise of land that came up to her shoulders; on the other was air as the land dropped off into a small tree- and rock-lined trench. In rainy weather, there was a stream that rushed through that trench, but right now there was nothing but debris in it. He'd crossed it earlier in his nightly rounds.

"Stay back, you beast," she threatened, stabbing at him with the stick for emphasis. "I might be little, but I know how to use this."

He chuckled again at the sight of the disheveled woman standing before him, holding the stick for all the world as if it would stop him.

She blanched at the sound of his chuckle, which to her ears must sound like a growl, and he saw the stick falter.

He wasn't sure what to do now. If he advanced toward her, he was pretty sure one of two things would happen. She would either stab him, or she would faint. Neither was an appealing prospect.

He decided the best course of action was to slowly back away, pretend his wolf pride hadn't been hurt by this little slip of a trembling woman with the big stick, and continue to follow her until she arrived safely in town. He could find out who the transgressing wolf was later on. His priority was her safety.

He realized suddenly that even if the first priority wasn't to ensure her safety, that was what he would do. The town had wanted her here —he was certain of it. He didn't know why, but Havenwood Falls periodically drew people in for reasons of its own.

He started backing up, his soft brown eyes meeting her terrified blue ones, and for just an instant, he saw a reaction in them that wasn't fear, but rather something indefinable like recognition. He felt the same flash of familiarity as if he knew her. But how could he? Where would he have met her before?

His heart pounded being this close to her. He was overpowered by her scent masked by her fear. He felt he knew her on a level that went beyond mere sight. She was his. His paw stopped mid-step.

That was it. She was *his*.

This was his mate?

This was the woman he'd been waiting for?

A human?

How was this possible? Yes, he'd asked the moon goddess for his mate, but . . . her?

Overhead, a crack of thunder sounded as if to agree with his realization. Then the rain came, cold, wet, and full of the promise of thicker moisture later. The girl, startled by the sudden onslaught, slipped.

With a delicate "*Oh*" of surprise, she disappeared over the side of the trail.

Rusty stared in shock for just a second, then bounded to the edge she'd fallen over.

She was nowhere to be seen.

The storm had swallowed her.

CHAPTER 5

*S*herry stared at the wolf, his teeth bared, the stick pointed at him. She knew it was a foolish gesture on her part. That weapon was hardly going to keep the large animal from charging at her, but she had to do something to protect herself. His brown eyes locked on hers, his teeth were huge and white in his snout, and she jabbed toward him with the stick in warning.

She fully expected him to charge, but he didn't. To her great surprise, he backed up, as if considering what to do next. For just a second, Sherry felt like she had a chance to survive this encounter. What a great story that would be for the grandchildren.

Sherry wasn't sure what to do next, either. Trapped on that thin trail, she cursed herself for running into the woods, not sure what instinct had sent her into the underbrush instead of running down the road. Worse yet, without a flashlight since she'd foolishly thrown it at the animal.

Now what?

Sherry felt the electricity in the air around her, surprised at the intensity of the tingling that set her nerve endings on fire. Glancing up, she saw the clouds scurrying across the sky, covering the moon and stars and obliterating almost all light. She narrowed her eyes, trying to see the wolf's shape in the total darkness. She still held the stick pointed in its direction, and she was certain it would leap at any second.

But nothing happened. Her breathing became rapid with fear, and her knees and arms trembled as she sought to remain calm in the face of this threat to her person.

Then, out of nowhere, the sky erupted into a thunderstorm of such intensity that, before she could move, Sherry felt the thin trail giving way. Reacting by instinct, she leapt to the side as the dirt under her feet began to crumble, but she was too late. She clawed nothing but air as her body fell into nothingness.

She crashed on rocks and trees and felt herself falling, end over end, down the side of the hill she'd been poised so precariously on. Her body crashed into another rock, head whipping back and cracking onto a thick tree. Still she continued to tumble down, rocks and dirt falling with her. Unable to grab onto anything to slow the fall, she cried out as she slammed into another rock hard enough that she blacked out.

So this is how it ends, she thought before darkness took her, *on the side of a hill in a place I never heard of before, with a wolf the only witness to my end.*

SHIT! Rusty shouted, his voice a howl of displeasure as he followed the woman over the edge of the trail and down the hill.

There was an eerie stillness as he followed her smell until he found her, bleeding from a deep head wound, at the bottom of the hill.

He whined and whimpered as he nuzzled her, trying to see if she still breathed. He was reassured she was still alive when she stirred slightly at the touch of his cold nose on her cheek.

Alive.

Breathing.

Now what? He couldn't run for help. Leaving her here would

mean she would be without protection, and if the rain kept up with the intensity it was falling right now, she would drown. She'd slid under a pile of logs and old trees that had followed her down the side of the hill to land piled up at the bottom with her in the middle of the tangle of logs and dirt.

He tried to pull her from under the logs by grabbing the collar of her sweatshirt in his teeth and tugging her out, but all that did, now that the ground was so damp, was cause the logs to shift, burying her deeper underneath them. Already the water was beginning to fill the trench. He let her go, careful to ensure her head was protected from the rainwater that crept closer to her body.

He would have to transform into his human form, but he had no clothes nearby. If she woke . . . well, that might be hard to explain.

For a few precious seconds, he considered his options. One, stay and continue, in his wolf form, to try to free her, dragging her out of harm's way until he could get to a stash of his clothes and return to "find" her and bring her to safety. Or two, transform and then bring her to safety without a stitch of clothes on and hope she didn't wake.

Whimpering at the cold water that crept up his paws to his knees, he realized there was nothing else he could do.

His decision made, Rusty closed his eyes. Forcing the change too quickly was always more painful than letting it happen naturally. Praying to the moon goddess, he felt the familiar surge of pain and tingling take over his body. He groaned as his body lost its protective coating of fur and the cold air rushed over his skin, searing him with icy pellets of rain and sleet as the storm slammed into him.

He stood, stretched, and cried in his humanness at the loss of his furred body. Looking through the rivulets of rain that ran down his face and body, he stared at the woman at his feet. She was still unconscious, and the water now reached up to her waist. The rain pelted down as he worked to shift her from her prison, the water now climbing with icy fingers up her body to cover her up to her armpits.

He realized he had only minutes before the water would cover her completely, and he worked feverishly to free her, finally breathing a sigh of relief when, with a loud sucking noise, the trees released her form to his grip.

Groaning, he pulled her, his muscles aching and sore from his efforts to free her, stretched to their limits. He lifted her from the mud and pulled her to his chest where her head landed with a soft *thump*. He breathed in the scents of earth, dead leaves, jasmine, and the humanness of her.

That was what undid him. Her humanness overwhelmed him, and for an instant, he just wanted to hold her, his body protecting her from the worst of the rain as he pulled her away from the place that had almost become her tomb. As he crab-crawled with her up the hill, away from the encroaching water, he dug his heels in and held her to him tightly. Breathing heavily, he calmed his body, adrenaline from the near disaster and rescue making him weak at the knees. He needed to rest for a minute before continuing the climb to the top of the hill. Along the way, he found her purse, which he slipped around his neck to ensure it wouldn't be lost again. He imagined, like most women, she'd be devastated if it'd disappeared.

He held her close, her form stretched down the length of his body. Holding her this way, he hoped to give her some of his body warmth and stop her from shaking. At least, that was the reason he used to convince himself that his contact with her held some necessity, and he wasn't just doing it because he liked the feel of her against his naked skin. Rusty concentrated to slow his breathing and his racing heart that seemed to speed up with her proximity. Just when he thought he had his body under control, she did the worst possible thing she could do.

She opened her eyes.

She stared at him in confusion, her hand traveling up his bare chest to rest near his pounding heart, and he felt an unfamiliar shiver of pleasure at her touch. For just a second, he wanted to lay her down and take her in the woods, just like this, in an animal way he'd never wanted a woman before. It took all his strength not to follow thought with deed.

Unfocused, pain evident in their depths, her eyes met his gaze, and she whispered a soft, "Are you an angel?" before closing them again. She moaned, whether in pain or not he wasn't sure, as he picked her up and carried her up the hill and back onto the trail.

An angel? Well, I suppose there are worse things she could have called me, Rusty thought as he quickly traveled toward his hidden clothes.

CHAPTER 6

*C*arrying her to where his clothes were hidden proved to not be as easy as he'd thought it would be. Whether because he was exhausted from his night prowls, or because he was battling the emotions that being near her roused in him, Rusty was trembling by the time he reached his destination.

He laid her down gently, checking once again to make sure her breathing was regular, and was relieved to find it was. He noticed the cut on her head still oozed blood, but not as badly as it had at the beginning. Overhead, the storm still raged, but here, the canopy of trees was thick enough that it protected them from the worst of the rain that was now turning to sleet and would soon become snow. He shivered in the chill damp air, wishing once again he were wearing his wolf pelt.

He quickly brushed away the layer of leaves and twigs that covered his waterproof backpack and unzipped it. He pulled out his clothes, dressing quickly with furtive glances at the woman, making sure she was still unconscious. He really didn't want to have to explain that she'd been carried through the woods by a naked man who had been the wolf who'd caused all the trouble in the first place. Oh, and then there was that bump on her head.

But now, he thought as he squatted down next to her, *what am I to do with her?*

His phone, retrieved from the bag, was not showing any reception, which was odd in itself, as he had often made calls from this part of the woods without difficulty. He had to believe that the storm probably interfered with the reception out here, even though weather had never affected it before.

Instead of panicking, though, Rusty considered what he should do next. Obviously, he needed to get her some help. She might have a concussion, or at the very least, a really bad headache when she woke. He was closer to his cabin than to town, but would she suffer too badly if he took her home and gave her first aid there? He could take her to town in his truck once she regained consciousness or he finished his rudimentary first aid on her wound. His hesitation to turn her care over to the doctor in town played at the edge of his thoughts, but he put aside the deeper consideration of his reasons for wanting to keep her with him.

Then he had a startling thought. *If she were not who she was, would I still want to bring her to my cabin?* He decided that was a thought best left for later.

Before Rusty could ponder any longer, the air around him dropped another few degrees. Snow fell, slipping like icy fingers down the collar of his shirt in an ever thickening cloud of whiteness.

He reached down and gently picked her up. Taking her to his cabin it would be. At least there they would be out of the elements, and he could call for help from Havenwood Falls. Getting her warm was his first priority. The head wound looked to have finally stopped bleeding, but her unconscious state still had him worried about the possibility of a concussion.

Carrying her was somehow easier now. He curled her body into his for warmth, and within a half hour, they'd traversed the distance to his cabin. In that short span of time, the intermittent flakes that had first fallen had become a mini-blizzard that had him wiping snow from his eyes as he walked, not an easy task as he carried her. Snow had accumulated along the path, and he left footprints behind him as he walked.

Hard to believe it was spring, but that was Colorado for you. Wait a few hours and the weather would change, the locals said. Today was definitely proof of the vagaries of Mother Nature's mind.

When he reached the cabin, he sighed in relief. The wood was stacked to the left of the door, and he noticed the rack was half full. He made a mental note to cut more. His front porch, holding two rocking chairs and a few half-hearted attempts at greenery that were just twigs in dirt right now, was the most welcome sight he'd seen in a while.

As he passed, he noticed his truck—a beat-up Ford issued by the park for his use as a ranger, the job he occupied in his human form—listing to one side.

"What?" he asked no one, inspecting it as he walked. One of the tires was flat. "Oh, that's great. How did that happen?" This would put a monkey wrench in his plans to take the woman into town.

They might just have to stay here for a few days after all. At least until he could get Joshua out here with either a tow truck or a new tire.

Once they entered the cabin, Rusty walked to the far end where his bedroom was and set her on the bed. After wrapping two layers of quilts around her, he left the room to find his first aid kit.

When he returned a few minutes later, he found her snuggled into the covers, snoring lightly. She looked adorable, and he couldn't resist reaching out and smoothing her hair off her face. She moaned at his touch, and he drew his hand back, afraid he'd hurt her. She muttered something under her breath, and he thought he heard the words "my angel" before she fell back into a fitful sleep. Watching her for a few minutes more, he felt a strong desire to join her under the covers. The thought of her body against his bare skin roused him once again to desire.

He treated her head wound as best as he could and bandaged it. She never moved under his touch. He rubbed her cheek, the feel of her silky smooth skin overwhelming him, and he had to draw back several times to maintain control over his body. He could still feel the wolf inside him.

Once her wounds were treated, he stepped from the room and closed the door, leaving it slightly open so he could hear if she stirred.

He shrugged into his coat and went outside to retrieve some wood for the fireplace. The storm had picked up in intensity. There was no way anyone was getting to his cabin tonight in this weather. His arms full of wood, he leaned down to the fireplace and settled the fire into a rush of flames. He tried to stop thinking about what might have happened had the woman continued to walk toward town in this storm, dressed inappropriately for the weather as she had been.

He set about preparing some leftover stew for dinner, hoping she might wake soon and knowing she would be hungry when she did. While he waited for the stew to cook, he checked his phone and noticed there was still no service. Now what was he to do?

This woman appeared to be on the mend, so once she woke up, he could check her for a concussion, but until then, he had to pray she was okay.

His thoughts turned to whom she might be as he settled into a chair near the fireplace. He picked up a book and read three pages without remembering a word. Keeping his thoughts off the woman and his strange reaction to her presence was not going to happen if this book couldn't hold his attention.

He stared into the flames and pondered this development.

Who was this woman? Why was she occupying so much of his thoughts? What had his strange need for her meant? Was he losing himself to his wolf side? Was his need for companionship as a human translating itself into animal desire when he was a wolf?

What would have happened if he'd given into those desires on the hillside when he'd held her in his arms? He shivered at the thought of the consequences of his actions if he hadn't been able to control himself.

What if she was his perfect mate?

There were consequences to that, too. Consequences that could do her more harm than good. Being with someone like him wasn't as simple as going to a justice of the peace to get married.

His eyes traveled to the room where she slept and widened in surprise.

She stood in the doorway, holding one of his guns, and it was pointed at him.

"Who are you?" she said in a soft voice, her hand trembling. "And what have you done to me?"

CHAPTER 7

*R*usty's first reaction was to hold up his hands. His second was to determine how many seconds it would take him to close the distance between them and disarm her. His third thought, and the best one he could come up with under the circumstances, was to play dumb.

"Ma'am?" he asked, trying to reassure her with his confused expression and non-threatening manner that he had no idea what she was talking about.

He studied the gun she held and then smiled slightly, knowing it wasn't loaded. But she didn't know that, and he had a feeling if he told her, she would be less than believing. He decided to let her think she had the upper hand.

"What. Am. I. Doing. Here?" she asked.

Her hand trembled, and her voice, brave though it was, was weak, indicating she was not fully back to her strength yet. He could overpower her in an instant if he needed to. He chose not to.

"Here, why don't you sit? I'll get us some stew. I think it's ready now."

"Where am I?" she persisted. She raised the gun, using two hands to hold it steady.

He ignored the weapon, pointing again to the chair. Rising, he carefully went to the stove and put the stew into two bowls. He set one on the table next to the empty chair and one next to his seat. Returning to the kitchen island, he cut a couple slabs of bread and put butter onto two plates, which also held a few strawberries and grapes he'd pulled from the fridge.

Once he was seated, he began eating, blowing on the food and taking a bite to let her know it was safe to eat. She eyed the stew, then him, and then the stew again.

"It's okay," Rusty reassured her.

The woman finally sat, shifting the gun to her other hand while keeping it pointed at him, and picking up the spoon for a taste of the stew. The moan that erupted from her lips surprised them both. She giggled, embarrassment pinking her face.

Rusty reached over and took the gun from her hand, and she gave it up without resistance.

"It's not loaded," he told her quietly.

"Oh," she said, looking at him with wide eyes. Rusty noticed they were a light blue ringed by a dark velvety blue like the twilight sky before true night fell. He liked them. These were eyes a man could get lost in, and find himself again.

"I . . . what happened to me?" she asked, as she buttered her bread.

"You were injured in a fall in the woods. I'm a park ranger for this forest. I was out on foot patrol and came upon you under some logs. I managed to pull you free and get you back here to my cabin before the full force of the storm hit."

"There was a wolf . . ." she said, her brow furrowing at the memory. "I remember seeing a wolf." She touched her forehead, her spoon clattering into the empty stew bowl. "And I remember . . . you?" She said that last as if it was a question.

He didn't answer, pretending to have a mouth full of stew instead.

"Was it you?" She looked at him with an intensity that made him blush.

"I suppose it was . . ." he finally admitted. "I did rescue you, after all."

"Thank you . . ." She hesitated. "But my rescuer was . . . different."

"How do you mean 'different'?" Rusty asked, wondering how much she did remember.

"Why did you bring me here?" she asked, changing the subject. She blushed, and Rusty silently cursed. How much did she remember?

"The storm," he explained. "I was walking in the woods, you see." Taking her bowl, he went to the kitchen and refilled them. "When I found you, I had to carry you someplace to get your wound treated. I decided it was faster to bring you here than try to take you to town since my phone wasn't working and calling for help wasn't possible. This was both a good thing and a not-so-good thing."

"Oh? Why's that?"

"Well, this storm for one thing. I had no clue it was going to hit with this kind of ferocity. It's already several inches thick in some spots and getting deeper, and my truck has a flat tire with no spare. Probably can't get anyone out here tonight just for a flat. We have plenty of food, so if your condition wasn't too bad, I thought we could just hunker down here and wait it out. I expect it will only last through tonight, maybe tomorrow. Then we can get you to town and have someone look at your wound. Although, I think it is okay."

"My phone isn't working either," she said. "My car died on the way to Havenwood Falls. I thought if I walked down the road a bit, I might find an area that was clear, and I could get reception and make a call. But it didn't...clear, that is."

Rusty grunted at her explanation.

SHERRY TOOK a moment to look around the cabin. The walls were uncovered, with not even a picture anywhere on the shelves. There was nothing personal at all in here that she could see. Its rustic walls were logs stacked on top of each other, reminding her of those Lincoln Log houses she'd built as a kid. She wondered if he'd built the cabin himself. It had the feel of the tender touch of someone's hands on it.

He did, however, have books scattered everywhere. Some were by popular authors she read herself, and others by people she remembered from her college days. There was a guitar in one corner, its surface oiled and gleaming. Obviously, he played it often. The bed she'd left had been covered by layers of quilts. Apparently, he spent a lot of time here in weather that was less than ideal.

Two kerosene lamps hung beside the door. There was also an axe, its blade down, resting against the wall.

The fire blazed and popped merrily in front of her, and Sherry felt herself relaxing as its warmth enveloped her. She had stopped shivering, the stew and inviting fire working wonders on her psyche. She blushed at the thought that she'd nearly shot him, thinking he had kidnapped her with evil intent, and then remembered the gun hadn't even been loaded. How foolish she'd been. If he'd wanted to harm her, he could have done so when she was unconscious, and who would've been the wiser? She had to stop comparing all men to her former fiancé. Not all men had secrets and ulterior motives.

"Who are you?" she asked, taking the second bowl of stew from him. She was so comfortable with him, now that she wasn't worried he was a murderer or worse, that she'd forgotten to ask for his name. How silly of her.

"Rusty…sorry, everyone calls me Rusty because of my red hair. My given name is Russell Higgins. Like I told you, I'm a park ranger, and this is my forest. And you?"

He looked at her out of the corner of his eye, as if her name didn't matter to him.

Sherry hesitated, dipping her bread into the stew before answering. How much should she tell him? Yes, he'd rescued her, but she only had his word that he was who he said he was. What if he really was a sick guy who lived in the woods kidnapping unsuspecting tourists? What if he'd brought her here for . . . for what, exactly? Even though she was oddly comfortable around him, what did she really know about him? Nothing. Not a darn thing.

She glanced around the cabin, once again reassured by the fact that there was nothing more dangerous here than an unloaded gun and an axe that was used to chop wood.

"Sherry Grimes. I'm a teacher—therapist really—in a school with children who have special needs. I work with children with disabilities. You know, like autism or Asperger's syndrome. I teach them how to cope with real-life situations before they are mainstreamed into a regular school."

"Around here?" Rusty asked.

"No," said Sherry. She took a long sip of water before continuing. "I work in a school out of state." She gave no further information.

"So, what brings you to our state? To Havenwood Falls?"

She laughed. "Chance?"

"Chance?" Rusty repeated.

"Yes. I was driving with no particular destination in mind. My school is on spring break right now, and I stopped at this information place, you know the kind where you pick up maps, go to the bathroom, or get snacks?"

He nodded.

"Well, while I was there, this nice old man suggested I visit Havenwood Falls. He gave me a flyer, and it had a number to rent cabins."

"Old man? Who was he?" Rusty's tone was curious.

"I'm not sure. He looked like he worked at the rest area, but when I tried to thank him, the woman working there acted like I was crazy. She said she didn't know who I was talking about. Now that I think about it, the whole thing was a little strange. But I did call the number on the flyer to rent a cabin. That much was normal."

"A cabin at the ski resort? Or at the vineyards?"

"No, it didn't sound like those. She said it was rustic, in the middle of the woods, up the mountain."

"Must be Melissa Richter's place, then. She owns a few cabins up the mountain. Was it her?"

"I guess so. She was very nice. I rented one for the next week. Well, I guess I need to cancel that, since I seem to be stuck here for a bit. Of course, I have no phone reception."

Sherry buried her head in her hands, releasing small sobs as her situation suddenly overwhelmed her. A few moments later, having cried herself out, he reached a hand toward her and said, "Whatever is bothering you, do you want to talk about it?"

Sherry shook her head. Getting up, she walked to the kitchen and rinsed out her dishes. Cleaning the counters took her mind off her thoughts. She wondered—and instantly hated herself for it—what Brad was doing right now. After scrubbing furiously at an invisible spot on the counter's surface, she finally threw the scouring sponge into the sink and stalked off toward the chair.

Rusty looked at her, but said nothing. For that she was grateful.

Unbidden, the image of the russet-skinned man entered her thoughts. She closed her eyes, willing the image of her angel from her mind. It was her imagination that a wolf changed into a man in front of her—a glorious man. *That is not possible.* The bump on her head had addled her brains, that was all it was. This was the real world, not a fantasy one.

How in the world could she possibly have been lifted up and carried in the arms of an angel back from death? Honestly, she needed therapy. Shaking her head, she stood and walked toward the bedroom.

Turning at the door, she asked, "Is there a bathroom in here, or do I need to go outside?"

He laughed. "Rustic as my cabin is, I, too, like some comforts. There's a small bathroom with a shower in the back of the bedroom."

He walked with her into the bedroom and pointed to the closed door at the far end of the room.

Eyeing the shower, Sherry sighed in pleasure. She felt horrible, covered in mud and debris from her time under the logs. It would be nice to be clean again.

"Can I . . .?" she pointed in the direction of the bathroom.

"Oh, of course." Rusty colored in embarrassment. "I'm sorry. I should have offered that to you as soon as you woke." Neither mentioned that she'd been pointing a gun at him at that time.

"I . . . have no clothes," Sherry said in sudden embarrassment. All her spare clothing was in her abandoned car.

"No problem. I'll see what I have that you can wear," Rusty said. "I have a washer and dryer, so if you'll leave your clothes outside the door, I'll throw them in while you shower."

"My blouse is silk." Sherry sighed. "It's probably ruined. Just throw it away. Cannot be washed, but the rest of my clothes can be."

"Okay. Just leave them outside the door."

Sherry slipped her clothes off, setting them outside the door as requested. She stepped into the shower, grateful for the spray of hot water that greeted her. She found soap and a washcloth inside the tub, along with a generic brand of shampoo that smelled delightfully of herbs, not too manly, and that surprised her. He struck her as a Head and Shoulders kind of guy. Just goes to show how wrong one can be.

Fifteen minutes later, she stepped out of the shower and grabbed a white towel that she wrapped around her body, and another, smaller one that she wrapped around her hair. Sighing in contentment, amazed at what a shower could do to revitalize a person, she stepped into the bedroom to find a pair of sweatpants, at least two sizes too big, fortunately with a drawstring, and an oversized T-shirt waiting for her. He'd also thoughtfully provided her with a thick sweater to wear over her shirt.

Sherry pulled them close to her, not surprised they smelled delightfully like him, woodsy and a bit musty, like a fur coat that had stayed in the closet too long. She decided she liked that smell. It smelled real. Not like Brad's cologne that smelled of stuffy boardrooms or what he liked to call "old money." Thinking of Brad made her mad again, and she stomped over to the far side of the bedroom to look out the window when she heard the sound of chopping.

She could see Rusty's trim figure in the squall that was still going full force outside. He was wearing a sweatshirt, and every time he raised his arms to bring the axe down, the fabric stretched across his back. She liked the view. Rusty's backside looked like it'd been molded into those jeans. His model-like good looks were obviously natural, not like Brad's, which were the product of expensive monthly trips to the spa that she paid for.

She chuckled as she wondered what Brad was going to do now that she was no longer footing the bill for his primping. He was a struggling actor—the struggling part coming from her juggling their bills to afford his wardrobe and mani-pedis, all of which had only garnered him a toothpaste commercial and walk-on part in a play—without a speaking role, mind you. It had been an off-off-Broadway play at best and had closed on the road after its stint in her town. Not that the play's closing could be attributed directly to Brad's part in the play, but still . . . she liked to think his bumbling entrance and exit as Bellboy #3 had had some small part in its disastrous run.

She calculated how much not having to pay those bills anymore would mean to her bank account and smiled as she realized she would finally be able to afford to travel at least once a year, something she'd been aching to do for ages. She'd put it off at Brad's insistence they stay close to home in case he got a call for an audition. Even though they didn't live in a place like Los Angeles, there was a thriving theater community in Albuquerque, and Brad's good looks were often needed for a role. Of course, now she wondered if his refusal to leave had to do with his bimbo. Not that it mattered anymore. She had never felt so free in her whole life.

Grinning widely, she waved at Rusty, who'd turned and waved to her.

She might be in the cabin of a stranger, but at least she was going to have some fun while she was here. When this weather cleared, she would go to Havenwood Falls and not regret one thing that might happen in between.

She almost skipped her way into the other room. She'd never felt this right about any decision in her life.

CHAPTER 8

*W*hen Rusty came back inside with an armful of wood, which he laid in the box next to the fireplace, Sherry was sitting in the living room again, freshly clean and a little distracting in his clothes. She'd somehow managed to find some popcorn he didn't remember having. She pointed to the television, but when they turned it on, hoping to watch a movie, only snow greeted them. He thought that was rather ironic—snow outside and snow inside. Not to be disappointed, Sherry suggested they play a game. He couldn't find anything that appealed to her.

Sighing, Sherry collapsed back into the chair, her disappointment and boredom evident in the droop of her shoulders.

Rusty couldn't stop staring at her. She was fascinating. From the way her hands moved, so delicate, like they were conducting the very air around her, to the way her eyes sparkled when she smiled. She wore her emotions on her sleeve, and he could smell them as if they were flowers. His house was full of so many interesting textures, but until she'd arrived, he'd never known he was missing out on any of it. No other woman had ever excited or awakened his senses like she did.

Her dark hair, a rich brown with golden highlights, drew his eyes to her every time she turned her head. The way her hair fanned out gently, like angel wings resting on her shoulders, made him want to reach out and touch the ends to feel how soft they were.

He wanted to explore every one of the hollows at the base of her neck. He wanted to bury his face in her skin, taste the magic that was her. He pulled his eyes away from her before he revealed his desire. He'd only just met her, and her first impression of him had been fear that he was going to harm her. He couldn't make that fear come true.

His eyes fell on his guitar, and he said, "How about some music?"

He wasn't' sure what drew him to do this, as he rarely played in front of friends, let alone a woman he was desperate to impress, but without her permission, he walked over, picked up his guitar, and brought it back to his seat.

"So, I'm not a professional," he said with a nervous chuckle, "but I will give it my best shot. Any requests?"

Sherry pulled her legs up under her and rested her elbows on her knees as she set her chin in her hands.

"Surprise me," was all she said.

He ran through his repertoire and tossed out a couple of the rowdier songs Joshua Breem, the local mechanic, and he liked to play together. Those were best left to days filled with beer and touch-football games. He tuned the guitar while he considered the options remaining to him.

Finally, he thought of the song he'd written a few years ago when, in a fit of loneliness, he'd first sent his wish up to the moon goddess. Strumming a few chords, he found the key and began.

"Here's one I wrote a little while ago," he said. "It's called, 'Before I Ever Met You.'"

Before I ever met you, the sky wasn't blue
The grass wasn't green, and my heart wasn't true
Before I ever met you, the oceans didn't come to shore
The waves crashed unheard, and the gulls cried no more
Before I ever met you, the night was dreary and dark
The day held no sun, my world was cold and stark
I was waiting for the possibility
Against all improbability

That you would find me
Your love would set me free
Before I ever met you, I cried myself to sleep
Prayers unanswered, dreams a wish my heart could keep
Before I ever met you, I was haunted by desires
Secrets unrealized, wishes tossed upon a funeral pyre
Before I ever met you, I waited for life to wake me
Then I met you and all doubts deserted me

AS HE STRUMMED the last chord, Rusty looked over, curious to see what Sherry thought of it. He was surprised to see her wiping tears from her eyes on the sleeves of the sweater.

"Sorry," she said in a voice thick with emotion. "That was beautiful."

"Thanks," he said. He continued strumming the strings, grateful for the distraction from his own emotions. He realized, casting another sidelong glance in her direction, that he wanted her to like that song. He *needed* her to like that song.

"Whom did you write it for?" she asked. She leaned forward, and the sweater, two sizes too big, fell open slightly at the neck, revealing her collarbone and the top swell of her breasts. He wanted to reach out and touch the smoothness of her skin right where it throbbed at the base of her throat and let his hand travel further down.

It took all his willpower to look away from her. Getting up from his chair abruptly, he set the guitar back in its stand, giving himself time to think how to answer that simple question. Whom did he write it for? He wrote it for a love he had never known. He wrote it for a love he was waiting for. He wrote it for . . . her.

And he realized that was true. She was the answer to his entreaty to the moon. But how would she take it if he told her that their meeting had been arranged by the supernatural, and not by a fall down a hill?

How would she feel about being chosen as his mate? If she would even have him, that was.

There was always the fear that mingling human and supernatural blood might cause problems in the future. There were people on both sides who were strongly against such unions and would not allow it, or at the very least would make their marriage difficult, but the fact remained that he was given very little choice in the matter. His wolf blood had chosen her, and he was bound as securely as a golden ring to her.

Surely the moon goddess had sent her to him. Why else would he be there at the exact moment she needed him most? Why else would she be here now, in his cabin, in the middle of a snow squall no one had expected or predicted? Surely this was fate, the answer to his prayer? But how could he tell her this?

She was a human after all, and not one who likely knew of the existence of supernatural beings. She wouldn't understand. She would hate him. She would be repulsed by what he was. He couldn't put her through that. He couldn't put himself through that.

No, no secrets would be revealed tonight. If she was to know his secret, he would have to move cautiously, bring her around to their fate slowly and with finesse.

Whom did he write this song for, after all? He wrote it for the one who would complete his life. He wrote it for the one who was to share his world.

She was the desire of his heart. She was his mate.

So how did he answer her question?

She stared at him with the calmest of expressions, as if she was innocent in all of this. And she was. She was very innocent. And yet, she was totally captivating and alluring.

So he said the only thing he could think of to say.

"I wrote it for someone I haven't met yet."

The disappointment in her face almost made him change his mind. Almost.

CHAPTER 9

Sherry knew he was lying. She couldn't have said why she knew it, but she was certain he had written that song for someone who mattered a great deal to him. She respected his right to privacy, but she felt oddly disappointed that he hadn't trusted her enough to tell her who it was.

And then she mentally kicked herself. Who was she, after all, to demand he bare his soul? They'd only just met. Of course, their meeting had been a bit unusual, and in a way, she felt strangely drawn to this taciturn man with so many layers. But in a few days, she would be on her way back to her old life far away, so why should she expect him to tell her anything that mattered as much as the woman he'd written such a beautiful song for?

The air in the room seemed charged with secrets, and it made her uncomfortable. Yawning, she decided it was time for her to go to bed.

"Um . . . where shall I sleep?" she asked, not sure he wanted her in his bed, but not seeing any other options in the small cabin. She supposed she could sleep in one of the chairs. They were big and comfortable, and she was fairly small. She hated the thought of Rusty, with his long legs and body, having to try to sleep in the chair, when it was her unexpected arrival that would put him out of his bed.

"Oh, you can have the bed," he assured her. "Let me just change the sheets. I'm afraid I wasn't comfortable changing you out of your clothes when you arrived, and there's some mud on the sheets."

Sherry blushed at the idea of this man removing her clothes and was relieved he had remained a gentleman. Then she remembered she'd accused him of intending her harm when she'd awoken and blushed even deeper.

Her eyes met his, and she saw a twinkle in their brown depths and a dimple in his cheek from a barely suppressed smile, letting her know he'd read her thoughts. Turning away, she said, "I can do that."

"It's no trouble, but we can get it done in no time if you help."

Nodding, Sherry followed him into the bedroom. He removed a set of sheets from the chest at the foot of the bed and set them aside as he began removing the quilts. Sherry took the top quilt from him and folded it, setting it on top of the chest. She did the same with the second quilt. Running her hand over them, she admired the tight stitching and beautiful patterns on each of them. She could tell they'd been hand-stitched by someone who took pride in their work, and she remarked on it in a voice full of admiration.

"These are beautiful. Who made them?"

Rusty hesitated, then finally said, "A friend from town. She was worried I might be cold out here all on my own."

"She did a wonderful job on these. I would love to get one. Does she sell them?"

Rusty paused again before answering. "She passed away."

"Oh, I'm sorry, I didn't mean . . ."

"It's okay. You couldn't have known. She was a dear friend. The wife of a dear friend. She had cancer."

"Oh, sorry." Sherry hated repeating herself, but she couldn't think of anything else to say. It was obvious this person had been someone dear to him, and she wanted to console Rusty.

Without realizing she was doing it, Sherry reached out and touched Rusty on the arm. His muscle tightened under her hand, sending tingles under her skin. What was it about him that excited her so? Sherry was confused, removing her hand almost immediately, and she stepped away. There was something deep in his eyes, something that drew her back to him.

Standing next to him, she looked up, reaching out to touch his arm again. Ignoring the tingling, she watched her hand slide up his arm as if her hand wasn't attached to her body. She felt him tense up. She looked at him as she moved closer until her body was almost pressed against his.

She saw a muscle twitch in his jaw, and her fingers touched the spot, warmth traveling up her body as his heat enveloped her. He smelled of musk and wood smoke, and she was suddenly aware of how little space separated them.

"I'm sorry . . ." She cursed herself again for saying that over and over. What did she have to be sorry about? She kept apologizing, not knowing why.

"Can you move slightly to the left so I can get the old sheets off?" His voice sounded so calm, but she had a feeling he was anything but. She smiled nervously and stepped away to give him more room, moving to the right instead of the left in her nervousness, bringing her up against his rock hard chest.

"Sorry . . ." she started to say again and then bit back the words.

He didn't move.

She didn't move.

They stared at each other, and she felt herself leaning into him even more, craving the warmth of his body. There was something primal in this need, something she didn't understand. Something she needed, wanted, and yet feared was about to happen. She knew she should step away, leave that room—that cabin—or she would never leave.

She couldn't move, though. Her feet felt rooted to the floor. She waited.

Finally, he groaned, and leaning down, he took her mouth with his, pushing into her with his tongue in a way she'd never been kissed before. She slipped her arms up around his neck, welcoming him into her embrace.

He ended the kiss after a blissful minute that she wanted to go on forever.

Looking at her, his eyes boring into hers, he said in a strangled voice filled with repressed emotion, "Are you sure this is what you want? You don't know what you are asking of me."

Sherry, eyes locked with his, nodded, not trusting herself to speak.

He lowered his head to hers, pushing her back onto the bed as he did so, his long form hot against her own.

Before she lost herself in his kisses, Sherry felt they had rather satisfactorily solved the dilemma of who would be sleeping in the bed.

CHAPTER 10

*L*ater, as the night lightened into day, Rusty woke to find his arm asleep under the still form of the woman he'd just marked as his own. He traced a finger along her jaw and down her throat, careful not to wake her. He wanted to remember her like this always. She was beautiful.

But her beauty was more than skin deep. Her dark hair was spread out on the pillow like a fan, framing her tiny face with its delicate cheekbones. He was amazed at how fragile she appeared, for her lovemaking had been fierce.

In spite of his wanting not to hurt her, she'd become ferocious in bed, begging him to love her with every fiber of his being. He tried to hold back, tried to keep from marking her as his own, but he couldn't. Her touch had set him afire, and her kisses had seared him to his soul.

While there was no outward change in either of them, he knew that she was marked now and would always be his, even if they never made love again. If he couldn't convince her to stay with him and accept his transformation into the wolf, he would never love another woman.

She was his.

More importantly, he was hers.

Forever.

There would never be another who could take him to the heights of love that the two of them had experienced last night. Their bodies, both naked and glowing from lovemaking, were cooling. He feared she might catch ill, so he started to move from the embrace of their bodies to get a blanket. That slight movement caused Sherry to rouse.

"Don't leave me," she murmured in a soft whisper, pulling his body back to hers with a possessiveness he found endearing.

She ran her fingers along his bare hip, her leg sliding between his, her body rising to meet his desire as she pulled him tighter to her.

He kissed her shoulder and whispered in her ear, "I need to get a quilt before we both freeze."

She laughed, her eyes still closed, her breath raising goose bumps on his skin that had nothing to do with the cold.

"Hurry, lover," she said as she caressed his chest with a finger. Her body promised more, and he quickly jerked a quilt over them, pulling her into its warmth as his mouth reached hers.

He sent a silent prayer of thanks to the moon goddess, because he had a feeling that all their tomorrows would bring nothing to match this night, and that all the nights that followed would pale in comparison.

Rusty woke later to the glare of sunlight through the window, an empty bed, and the smell of coffee. For just a minute, he was disoriented.

"Hello, sleepyhead," said a voice from the doorway.

Rusty turned over to see Sherry, wearing nothing but his overlarge sweater and carrying a tray on which she had placed two plates heaped high with eggs and toast, and two cups of steaming coffee.

He wasn't sure which he was happier to see.

He smiled seductively at her. "What's all this?"

"This," Sherry said, setting the tray down carefully on the chest at the foot of the bed, "is a thank you breakfast for my rescuer."

"Oh?" Rusty took the coffee cup she offered him. The sweater lifted up slightly as she leaned over, revealing her very pert backside.

He admired the view without apology. He remembered the feel of that flesh as he'd cupped it in his hand the night before, his lips curling in a satisfied smile.

"Do you often make thank you breakfasts?" he said to distract himself from wanting her again.

"Nope, this is the first one," Sherry admitted as she tapped her coffee cup against his in a silent toast. Taking a sip, they looked at each other with unabashed hunger.

"The storm has nearly stopped," Rusty said, looking out the window. He tried to keep his voice light. "I think there might be reception on our phones now. I can call for someone to come for you, if you would like me to."

"In that much of a hurry to have me leave, are you?" Sherry quipped. She turned her face away, so he had to pull her around by the chin to regain her attention.

"That's not it at all. I just thought you might like to continue with your vacation. This," he pointed around the room, "might be a part of your trip you might not want to remember in the light of day." He kept his tone light, even though his heart was breaking. He couldn't let her know. He'd decided that revealing his secret to her might not be the best idea right now.

SHERRY NODDED. Handing him the rest of the breakfast she had prepared, she considered his comments. She had come here to get away from romantic entanglements, and what had she done the very first chance she'd had? Jumped in bed with a very sexy park ranger. In what way had that solved anything?

She realized Rusty was just a rebound guy and that their encounter had no lasting consequences or expectations for either of them, but she felt oddly disappointed that he could dismiss her so easily. She touched her head. The wound was sore, but not too painful, and she'd had no headache to speak of, so thankfully she'd been spared a concussion, but

Sherry found herself trying to think up excuses to stay here a little longer.

She could pretend she was still too ill to travel, but her lovemaking last night made that lie a little thin. She blushed, remembering how enthusiastic she'd been in bed. She'd never been that free with Brad, and perhaps that was why he'd felt the need to seek comfort in the beds of other women. She immediately dismissed that self-deprecating thought. Brad's infidelities were not her fault, and she would stop blaming herself.

"I suppose I do need to call someone. At least to cancel the cabin up the mountain. I have a feeling the road will be impassable."

Rusty nodded, taking a sip of coffee. "With my truck out of commission, I have to call my friend Joshua, so I think he can give you a ride to town after picking up your car. He's the town mechanic as well as the tow truck driver. He can take you to the Whisper Falls Inn, which I think would be the best place for you to stay in town. The inn has fallen on hard times, but is still a beautiful Victorian manor with a lot of character, and its new owner, Michaela, is working hard to put it back to its original condition. You'll like it very much."

"Okay," Sherry said, hating how flat her voice sounded. She was disappointed he wasn't fighting to keep her here, but oddly understood. He was a man who liked living alone. She got that.

"I'll get my clothes if you'll call your friend?"

"Sure," Rusty agreed. He seemed to want to say something else, and Sherry held her breath, hoping he'd say what she wanted to hear, but he didn't. He offered her the shower first, slipping out of bed.

His nakedness in the light of day caused Sherry to gasp. He was magnificent, an Adonis of the forest, and she would forever be comparing future boyfriends to his lean, muscular form and finding them lacking.

If he felt her admiration, Rusty made no mention of it. He slipped on a pair of sweatpants and walked into the other room. She appreciated his kindness in giving her time to pull herself together. A minute later, he returned with her clothes, neatly folded, which he handed to her before taking the tray and cups to the other room.

As the door closed behind him, Sherry let the tears fall that had been prickling at the back of her eyes. She sobbed in the shower, letting the warm water run over her body, hoping it would wash away her desire as easily as it washed away his touch.

CHAPTER 11

*R*usty listened to the shower and tried to keep his emotions in check. All he could imagine was the feel of her body against his. He cursed the moon goddess for sending him the one woman he could never keep. Putting her in his bed had been the cruelest of jokes.

He found his cell phone. Relieved to see several bars lit up, he called Joshua and in a few words, explained to his friend what was needed. Joshua agreed to attempt the trip to his cabin to help with the tire.

"The roads are still a bit treacherous," Joshua said cautiously, "but I'll set out in about an hour."

Rusty hung up and was just finishing the call to Melissa Richter when Sherry came into the kitchen. Dressed, she looked less like the woman who'd warmed his bed and more like the stranger he'd met in the woods. He felt their separation keenly. But outwardly, Rusty gave no sign of his broken heart.

He supposed it was a good thing she'd changed back into her own clothes, because if he'd had to send her out in his sweater, he wasn't sure he could control his actions. He was already fighting to keep his desires in check.

"I'm ready. When will your friend arrive?" She played with the strap of her purse in her nervousness.

"Joshua said it would be about an hour. He'll come here first, and we'll fix the tire. After that, he'll drive to your car, and then take you to town. I was just getting ready to call over to the inn to reserve you a room."

He picked up his phone and pulled up the inn's number. In a few minutes, he'd secured Sherry a room. Nothing else needed to be said, and the silence between the two grew louder than a jet airplane. Sherry went to the living room and sat down while she waited.

When Joshua pulled up, his truck loud in the stillness of a snow-blanketed world, Sherry nearly jumped up. At the sound of his footsteps on the porch, she met Rusty's gaze and then lowered her eyes. She wasn't sure what to say, so said nothing.

Joshua knocked, entering when Rusty called out to come in. Stepping inside the room, the other man looked between the two, eyebrow raised, and stomped his boots to remove the snow.

"Well, I reckon we can get that tire taken care of first. I brought a replacement. You got the jack?" He glanced over at Rusty, who nodded.

"You must be Miss . . .?" Joshua said, extending a hand to Sherry.

"Sherry Grimes," she said, introducing herself to the mechanic.

Sherry found his handshake firm and brief. He looked like a man who liked to keep things simple, and the silent exchanges between the two men were a little disconcerting. It was as if they had a secret language, one she had no clue how to speak, let alone understand.

"Okay, well, let's get that tire fixed. Then I will take the little lady into town."

He was out the door as soon as the words were out of his mouth.

Sherry looked at Rusty, who was shrugging into his coat. Pulling gloves from his pocket, he nodded toward the kitchen. "There's fresh coffee if you want a cup before you go. This shouldn't take long, and then you can be on the road."

Sherry raised her hand as if wanting to reach out to him, but nodded instead. Turning away, she walked toward the kitchen. Closing her eyes, she forced unshed tears back. Letting Rusty see her regret to be leaving would serve no good purpose.

A short while later, both men returned to the house. Sherry offered Joshua a cup of coffee, which he declined.

"Never touch the stuff," he said gruffly, "but I thank you kindly for the offer. You ready to go? The storm's coming back, I think. Best we get your car and get you to the inn."

Sherry nodded. Stepping past Rusty, she was careful not to touch him, but the urge to squeeze his arm was strong. A kiss in parting wouldn't have been out of order, but he didn't offer, and she wouldn't beg.

As she stepped up into the truck, she resisted the urge to look back.

Joshua backed out the truck, his gears grinding as he moved the large truck down the rutted drive. The air was growing cold again. Just before they rounded the corner to turn onto the main road, Sherry caught sight of Rusty out of the corner of her eye.

He stood on the porch, leaning against the post as he watched them disappear.

"He's a good . . . man, our Rusty," Joshua said, glancing over at her. "You can trust him. You can always trust him with . . . whatever needs trusting."

Sherry shot him a quick glance. Was her broken heart that obvious?

"My wife trusted him. She was dying of cancer when they met. They became instant friends. Best decision we ever made was to move to Havenwood Falls. Best decision I ever made was to marry my Evelyn in spite of . . . well, in spite of our differences, I guess you could say. I wouldn't trade a minute of the time we had together to be with anyone else."

Sherry nodded at him, confused about what he was really telling her. What did he mean by "differences"?

Before she could ask him for an explanation, they came to her car. It was covered in snow, but otherwise just as she'd left it. Could it only have been last night? So much had happened since that fateful decision to drive down a deserted road in a less-than-perfect car.

"You stay in here where it's warm, miss. I'll get the car in gear. May I have your keys?"

Sherry dug around in her purse, pulling out the keys and handing them to him. His gloved hand gripped hers for a second, forcing her to look at him.

"It'll all be okay, miss. If there's one thing my Evelyn was always right about, it was that the moon takes care of her own."

Sherry looked at him in confusion. What in the world was he talking about?

In a little over half an hour, they were back on the road and headed toward town. He'd first tried to start the car, but it was still not running, so he'd pulled her bag from the trunk before loading her car onto the truck's bed, and the bag now rested at her feet.

Joshua dropped Sherry off at the Whisper Falls Inn and told her he'd call her with the verdict on her car.

"Don't you worry, miss," he said before closing the door. "We'll have you back on the road and out of Havenwood Falls in no time. That is, if that's what you truly want."

Nodding to her, he continued on down the road.

"What an odd thing to say," Sherry muttered as she watched him go, her car traveling away from her. She hoped the damage wouldn't be too much, and at the same time, she hoped the repairs would take a few more days.

"Hello, are you coming in?"

Sherry turned at the sound and smiled at the young woman who stood on the porch. Glancing around the town, Sherry was struck by how much she liked its quaint shops and houses. This was the kind of town she'd always wanted to live in. It felt like it could be home.

Pulling her suitcase behind her, she walked up the steps and into the inn.

The smell inside the building was warm. The yeasty scents of freshly baked breads mixed with the smells of fresh wood and paint from the remodeling work in the lobby, and she felt instantly comfortable here. She wasn't disappointed in the room, either. It was occupied by a bed, a dresser, a desk with a phone on it, and a comfortable chair with a lamp nearby. There was a large window at one end of the room that looked out over a small garden.

She set her bag on the floor at the end of the bed and sat on the bed. In seconds, she had laid her head on the pillow, pulled up another beautifully quilted blanket, and let loose the tears she had been holding back all day.

Wrapped in the warm quilt, she cried away all her hurts. Old wounds had a way of creeping up at the worst of times. This was one of them.

CHAPTER 12

*B*rad looked at the woman asleep in the bed next to him and sighed. It was time for her to go, but he wasn't sure exactly how to get the bitch out of his house. She'd practically moved in once Sherry had left in such a tizzy. He knew she assumed she would take Sherry's place, but he found that idea less appealing than he once might have.

He'd met her in a strip club after another failed audition. At a low point, he'd invited her back to his house after they'd spent the night doing it in the back of his car. He'd taken her to breakfast, and then, knowing Sherry would be at work, brought her back to their house.

Well, Sherry's place actually, since she paid the rent on the small apartment they'd been living in together for the last six months.

He assumed she'd drive around and come back like a dog with its tail between its legs. But she hadn't, and now he was beginning to worry. It didn't help that he was stuck with this chick—Stephanie? Doris? Amanda? He couldn't remember her name, didn't even try. These days he just called them all "baby," and so far none had complained.

He usually only dated women he knew wouldn't want more than his body, which he was happy to donate to the cause of making women happy, but this one seemed to want the whole package. Not likely.

He needed his space. He'd thought Sherry understood that. In his roles as a model and sometimes actor, he needed to be footloose and fancy free. He'd thought Sherry was just a fling, something to fill the time in between jobs. She was fun, and smart, and seemed to really care about him, but his need for a walk on the wild side had doomed them.

Now he regretted it. The idea that the grass wasn't always greener on the other side was true. He needed to get her back.

Looking at the woman in the bed next to him in the cold, harsh light of day, he realized her boob job was sagging, her legs had been subjected to lipo so many times the cellulite had pock marks, and her wrinkles were not as appealing as they were in the darkness.

He slapped her hip harder than he intended and shoved her to wake her up.

"What's wrong, baby?" she asked him with what she probably thought was an adorable sexy pout, but which disgusted him now.

"Nothing's wrong. You need to get up. Get out of here. I got stuff to do. Come on, move it."

She sat up, calling him every name in the book in words of four letters and more. He ignored her. He walked like a cat stalking its prey toward the living room where he kept a pack of cigarettes hidden in a vase. Finding them, he lit up, even though he knew Sherry hated the smell of cigarettes in the house.

He'd told her he quit, but it was a lie.

Like so many other lies he'd told her. They all blended together into a jumble in his mind.

"Bitch," he whispered in the empty room.

"Hey, baby, when can I see you again?" The bimbo stood in the bedroom door, her blond hair disheveled from sleep, her lips pouty and full. He thought about taking her there, on the floor, before she left, but quickly dismissed the idea.

No sense giving her the idea she had a chance of getting back with him.

Instead he pointed to the door and silently sent her on her way.

She turned angry eyes in his direction, giving him the finger before the door closed on her.

She was already a memory to him, though.

Watching through the window as she left, his thoughts turned to Sherry. Where was she? Why hadn't she come crawling back yet? How was he going to find her?

Then he had a flash of brilliance. At his last audition, he'd sat next to a private investigator, someone with the ability to trace vehicles. What if he reported Sherry's car as stolen and had him trace it? Now, where did he put that guy's card?

A short while later he'd found the card and was chortling with glee to think of the surprise on her face when he showed up to surprise her. He imagined the reunion, which would involve a lot of time under the sheets, because the insult he'd thrown at her about being a bad lay was a complete lie. She was definitely *not* a bad lay. She was probably the best lover he'd ever had, and it had taken her running away to prove that to him.

In twenty minutes, he was connected to the private investigator and detailed his problem.

"It'll take a little time," the PI told him. "I'll get back to you when I know something. That'll be $200 for a motor vehicle trace. Fifty up front, and the rest when the information is found. Agreed?"

Brad hesitated—he had exactly $350 in the bank—but he was certain Sherry would be happy to repay him once he'd won her back. He could tell her it was "research" for his next role.

"Yep, that would be great."

A little while later, dressed in a pair of running shorts and a shirt in his signature black, Brad stretched before heading out for a jog. Keeping his body in great shape was important, and no matter what else was going on, he was not going to miss out on his run.

As he was undressing for his shower, his phone rang.

"Hello?"

"Got that information for you," the voice on the other end of the line said. "Car is at a place called Havenwood Falls. It's in Colorado.

There seems to be no address for the garage, just some vague directions to it. I think they have a bus that you pick up at a place nearby. Here's where you can pick up the shuttle."

Brad wrote down the address. "Got it, thanks."

Per the agreement, Brad paid the bill, wincing at the depletion of his bank account.

"Well, well," said Brad with a huge grin, "gotcha. See you soon, Sherry, my girl."

Time for a road trip.

CHAPTER 13

*R*usty felt the emptiness in the cabin as soon as the door closed behind Sherry. He stripped the bed, but as he stood in front of the washer, he couldn't bring himself to put the blankets into the machine.

Instead, he pulled them closer to his face and breathed in the deep rich smell of their lovemaking, reliving it all over again like a movie.

The feel of her skin, soft and fragrant with their friction, was almost more than he could bear to relive, but he needed to, wanted to. Wanting her was an ache in his soul so deep that it struck him in his bones. It was both pain and pleasure, joy and agony.

Knowing she was his mate, and knowing he could never force her to be with him, was driving him insane. He paced the cabin like one possessed, and when he had time to think about it rationally, he kicked himself for his hesitance in telling her the truth.

She was human, he rationalized. She wouldn't understand; she would have thought he was a freak. She wouldn't have wanted him, not the way he needed her to. He wouldn't take her pity. He wanted her wholly, body and soul.

Why had the town brought her here?

He wanted to talk to someone about it, and when Joshua had arrived, it had seemed the perfect chance to let down his guard. He'd known Joshua for a long time. Joshua had been married to Evelyn, a shifter like Rusty, even though Joshua was a human. Until the cancer had taken her, the two had been inseparable upon meeting. Joshua had been able to accept Evelyn's uniqueness without question, his love for her deep and forgiving.

The two had never kept secrets from each other, their love in the open for all to see. Their union had, while producing no children, been a very satisfying one, the kind of relationship Rusty hoped to have one day with his own mate.

But Sherry was special. She was a human who had no experience with supernatural or shifter beings. She was probably not even aware supernaturals existed, and had he revealed his true nature, it would have been a great shock. They'd only just met. He couldn't dump that on her.

Rusty knew this was true, but it still didn't take the pain away. He needed to shift, to run in the woods, to become the wolf. He could feel the need driving him mad with desire to race, to rend something apart. His emotions were so raw, so on edge, that he feared what might happen if he did change.

"Don't give in to it, Rusty," Joshua had cautioned him. "If you do, you'll regret it. You cannot let it control you. You must control it. You are too dangerous right now. Raw emotion leads to poor decisions."

Rusty had nodded, realizing his friend was trying to help him, but still hating the need for caution when his heart and body wanted him to do the most irrational thing he could think of, convince Sherry to stay with him…forever. But was love ever rational? Add to that the urgency of a mating denied, and you have the recipe for a disaster.

"I want to tell her how I feel," Rusty confessed. "But I sense she is raw from something emotional in her own life, and I'm afraid it will destroy her if I tell her what I am."

Joshua paused before speaking again. "When Evelyn and I talked about her change, the way she had to separate her two lives to be with me, the one thing we agreed on was that we would always be truthful. Secrets cause pain. Truth, while it may cause pain, too, is much kinder in the end."

"But my truth is the kind that people—those who are not supernaturals—don't understand. Their view of us is warped by television, movies, and books that depict us as killers with no control over our emotions and needs."

"That's true," Joshua had agreed. "In the end, I guess it all comes down to trust. Do you trust her to keep your secret? To understand *who* you are? Not *what* you are?"

"How did you and Evelyn reconcile this?"

Joshua smiled crookedly, the pain of Evelyn's death still written in his friend's face, and Rusty regretted mentioning her name.

"I loved her. That's all I needed to know. The rest was just window dressing. I wanted to be with her, and who she was inside mattered more to me than anything else. Give Sherry that chance, that choice, to make the decision. You won't regret it."

Rusty was still thinking about that as night fell and he prepared to go out on his nightly prowl.

Going to the end of the drive, he set off into the woods with thoughts of Sherry on his mind. The moon was high and bright tonight. Reflecting off the snow, the moonlight lit his way on his rounds.

He found himself on the edge of town, not a normal part of his route, and he knew why. Unable to stop himself, he crept along until he was at the back of the Whisper Falls Inn. Standing in the shadows, he looked up at the large, Victorian manor, wondering which window was the one to Sherry's room.

He saw one room at the far end overlooking the garden with its light on. Was that where she was? Was she unable to sleep, too? Was she thinking of him? He sent a silent message to her, hoping she was comfortable and would soon be asleep. And then, as if thinking about her had conjured her up, she was standing at the window.

He stared, willing her to see him, and fearing that if she did see him, she would guess his secret. He stepped from the shadows for just a brief second and then slipped back into darkness, heading toward the woods.

The night was uneventful, for which he was grateful. After the recent library fire, which was suspected to be arson, and the body he'd discovered in the woods near Wylie's Gulch a few weeks ago, he was glad to have found nothing out of the ordinary tonight. He turned back toward home, feeling better just being out in his beloved woods. As he loped along the side of the road, he heard the sound of a motor. Leaping quickly from the road, he crouched down as the shuttle passed and behind it, a car.

He saw a man, hunched over the wheel, his blond hair spiked in a style that was fashionable in movie stars and other celebrities. He was driving slowly, weaving slightly as if tired, and Rusty paused, something about the guy setting off warning bells in his mind.

Following him a short distance to make sure he didn't have trouble on the road, Rusty watched as the man rounded another corner and disappeared into the lights at the edge of town.

What was this fellow doing in Havenwood Falls?

CHAPTER 14

*S*herry tossed and turned in bed, unable to get comfortable. Nothing she did made her sleepy. She tried reading one of the books Michaela had loaned her, but she couldn't concentrate. She tried a warm shower, but that just made her think of Rusty and his cabin.

She tried warm milk and a chocolate chip cookie, which Michaela had brought to her room, but that just made her less tired, not more.

Finally she stood up, her restlessness a surprise to her. She was exhausted. She should have been asleep hours ago, but here she was, pacing her room. She finally felt herself drawn to the window.

Looking down, she saw the garden, still and silent in the night. Her eyes were caught by movement at the edge of her vision. A large dog, or possibly a wolf, sat on its haunches watching the inn. She felt a shiver, but not of fear. Rather, she felt a familiarity with the wolf.

Raising a hand to her forehead, she touched the small bandage she'd replaced earlier that night and then watched as the animal slipped back into the shadows and she lost sight of it.

Was it a dog? Or was it something else?

She continued to stare out the window for several minutes, but the creature never returned.

Finally, exhausted, she fell into bed and slept the night through, her dreams populated by a wolf that became at various times an angel and a man.

CHAPTER 15

*D*riving into town so late, Brad's options for lodging were limited. The lights of the Whisper Falls Inn were dark, indicating they were not welcoming guests at this hour, so Brad drove to the nearest motel where he got a room for the night.

The clerk grumbled and made pointed remarks to the time, but Brad ignored him. Paying with a credit card, he had to think if he still had any room left on it. Sighing in relief when the card went through, he took the key and went to his room.

Throwing his bag on the bed, he lay down, careful to stay on top of the covers. He didn't need to catch anything while here, and who knew who had been in this room—and doing what—before he'd arrived. He hoped Sherry would appreciate the effort he made to get them back together.

Falling asleep, he dreamed of the reunion the two would share when they met again. He was sure she was staying someplace better than the rathole his limited funds provided him.

CHAPTER 16

The next morning, Sherry woke up and headed downstairs. The first thing she needed to do was buy some new clothes. She couldn't wear half of what she'd grabbed when she had run from her fiancé's indiscretion. She definitely needed some new shoes.

She liked Michaela, the young woman who managed the inn. If she were to stay around, Sherry had a feeling the two women would become great friends. Michaela was always busy running the inn, and with all its remodeling needs, it made her time to visit pretty limited. Sherry felt guilty keeping Michaela from what she needed to do, so she curtailed her interruptions as best she could.

Pointed in the right direction by Michaela, she found herself at Backwoods Sport & Ski, the local outdoor shop where she picked up some jeans, sweaters, and a new sweatshirt with "Havenwood Falls" emblazoned across the front and a ski jump and ski slope in the background. Complete with thick socks and hiking boots, she felt like a new woman in her new clothes. She had also picked up some mittens, a hat, and a scarf in her favorite shade of blue. She almost felt like dancing down the street.

She made her way past the shops that wrapped around three sides of the town square's park. The area appeared to be vibrant and thriving. Everything smelled fresh and clean, the storm having added an edge of pine-scented air to the normal smells of coffee and fresh baked goods that captured her attention. She turned toward the smell of coffee, intending to purchase a cup, but stopped to admire the view of the street first.

Nodding to a few early morning risers like herself, she was surprised when they smiled and waved back before moving on to their activities. It made her feel welcome. A woman, jogging by in a bright purple track suit, waved and smiled like the others, as if greeting an old friend. Sherry waved back, a smile turning up the corners of her mouth.

As she wandered the streets, she marveled at how the brightly painted shops blanketed with freshly fallen snow from last night's storm added to the Currier & Ives appeal of the town. After a short time, she found herself in front of the Havenwood Falls Garage and decided to check on the progress of repairs to her car.

"Hey, Joshua," she greeted the mechanic. "Any word on my baby?"

Joshua turned, caught sight of her, and waved before walking toward her. He wiped his hands on a rag. Shaking her hand, he gestured for her to join him in his office.

"I was just starting on your car, so no definite word yet, but I think part of the problem is some loose wiring. For sure you have a busted hose, which I have replaced. I'll know more later today."

"Great," Sherry said with a smile. She sent up a silent prayer to whatever gods looked out for cars that the damage to her bank account wouldn't be too serious.

"Sherry," Joshua said, stopping her from leaving the shop, "I wonder if I might have a word with you?"

"Sure," said Sherry. "Is it about the car?"

"No, it's about our conversation yesterday."

"Oh." Sherry wanted to say that she would not discuss Rusty, but she had a feeling Joshua needed to say something important to her, and her therapy training kicked in.

Sitting back down in the bright red plastic chair, she faced him. This time it was Joshua who looked uncomfortable. She kept silent, waiting for him to open the conversation.

"I may have overstepped my boundaries, and for that I apologize. Sometimes I cannot help but interfere. It's my curse, Evelyn used to say."

Sherry smiled, waving a hand as if to say it was okay, but Joshua continued.

"This town has its secrets, and it's not my place to tell them, but I think you need to talk with Rusty. I think you need to know . . ."

"Know what?" asked Sherry, her tone sharper than she'd intended. She'd managed not to think of the sexy park ranger for the last hour, and here Joshua was, dragging her back down that road again.

"Just . . . talk to him."

And that was all the mechanic would say. He promised to call her as soon as he knew what was wrong with her car, and then he walked her to the door.

As the door closed behind her, she shook her head. Joshua was an odd one. She had no intention of following his advice. Rusty had had his chance to explain himself before she left, and he'd chosen not to. She had nothing more to say to him.

Walking back to the inn, distracted by her thoughts and not paying attention to where she was going, Sherry bumped into someone. Raising her eyes, an apology on her lips, she stared in shock.

"Well, hello, stranger," Brad said. He held her by the arms and gazed intently into her eyes, gauging her reaction.

"Brad?" she said, recovering her voice.

A truck passing by stopped quickly, before pulling up next to her. She heard the door open and close, but didn't take her eyes off Brad to see who it was.

"Sherry, is this man bothering you?" Rusty's voice penetrated her shocked mind.

"Mind your own business, stranger. This is my fiancée." Brad gripped her arms tighter.

"Sherry, is this true?" The hurt in Rusty's voice cut into her like a knife.

Glancing over at him, she hesitated then nodded. "Yes . . . I mean, no . . ."

Brad glared triumphantly at Rusty and then stared at her in consternation.

Rusty stared pointedly at Brad with his arms crossed and stepped closer to the pair.

Both men stood there, glowering at each other. Sherry felt like the pickle in the game of pickle in the middle.

"Is he or isn't he your fiancé?" Rusty pressed her, not taking his eyes from Brad.

"He was, but now he's not," Sherry said, ignoring Brad's strangled cry of anger.

"Yes, I am. I've come to ask you for your forgiveness," Brad insisted. He hadn't released her arms yet.

"Let her go," Rusty said softly, the threat of bodily harm implied in his tone of voice.

Brad released her.

Sherry stepped around both men, unable to stand the proprietary, testosterone-fueled glares that passed between them. She wasn't sure which one was more dangerous, and she didn't intend to find out.

Brad, seeing her leave, made as if to follow, but she heard Rusty warning him to stay away.

"Not sure who you are, cowboy," Brad said through clenched teeth, "but you'd better back off. That's *my* woman there. And I intend to take her home with me."

Before Sherry could protest his unjustifiable, territorial alpha attitude, Rusty moved toward Brad with clenched fists. His expression dark, Rusty said, "Don't you think you should ask her what *she* wants?"

Sherry reached out, her hand on Rusty's arm, stilling his anger for the moment. He shot her a quick glance, then returned his expression to Brad. Sherry pulled her arm away, but not before Brad noticed it.

Brad, awareness dawning in his eyes, darted a quick look between Sherry and Rusty and smirked. "I see. Sherry, is there something you need to tell me, sweetheart?"

Sherry threw up her hands in annoyance. "Stop it, Brad. Stop it, Rusty. Both of you, just stop being children. I belong to no one, Brad."

Rusty moved toward Brad, every muscle tight with the effort of holding back from physical violence. Sherry reached out. Touching Rusty on the arm once more, she felt his muscles relax, and she pulled her hand away again. Rusty's glare remained focused on Brad.

With a disgusted sound, Sherry walked away from the two men. They paid her no attention, neither man reacting to her departure.

When she reached the gate to the inn, she turned and saw Brad and Rusty arguing. Rusty, facing her, locked eyes with her, and she was surprised to see longing and regret in them.

She quickly turned away and walked up the stairs to the inn, closing the door firmly behind her.

Two hours later, Brad showed up at the inn to take her out to dinner. Sherry wanted to decline, but she was starving and dinner at the inn wouldn't be served for at least another hour. She knew Brad would just follow her anywhere she went, so against her better judgment, Sherry left with him. Throughout dinner, he kept trying to convince her he'd changed, that he wouldn't cheat on her anymore, that he loved her.

"Come on, baby," he'd said, taking her hand and raising it to his lips. "You know I mean it. I love you. I truly do."

Sherry was disgusted by his attempts to woo her. He was clumsy, and all she kept thinking about was how Rusty had never lied to her, that his emotions were always out in the open. She knew he could be trusted.

"Brad, it isn't just the blonde, or even the cheating, that has me thinking it is time to end our engagement. You barely pay anything toward our bills, and I pay all your bills, too. I cannot keep doing this. We are too different. You lie, and think everything is okay if you say you're sorry, but it's not okay."

"All right, I get it, you're hurt. But honey, what other choice do you have? I'm here, I'm what you need. You know this."

"No, Brad, it won't work. I want you out of the house when I get back. I won't do it anymore."

He stared at her with narrowed eyes. "It's that ranger, isn't it?"

Sherry looked away, her blush revealing everything.

"You slept with him, didn't you? And you talk about me being easy," he said bitterly.

Sherry stared at him with cold eyes. "It's over, Brad. I won't discuss it with you any further. I'll be home in three days. I want everything you own out of the house when I get back. And if you dare take anything of mine, I'll have you in court so fast, your head will spin."

"He'll never love you like I love you," Brad spat out as he stood up.

"I hope not," Sherry muttered under her breath. She wasn't even embarrassed by the temper tantrum Brad was causing as he stomped from the restaurant, promising revenge.

"You okay, miss?" the waiter asked when he brought her the check.

Sherry appreciated the waiter's concern, but wanted to leave as quickly as possible. Stepping outside, she remembered too late that Brad had driven them to the restaurant, since her car was in the shop one more day.

"Damn," she said, fumbling in her purse for her phone. She wondered if they had Uber in this neck of the woods, but doubted it.

"Need a ride?"

Sherry's head jerked up at the sound of Rusty's voice.

Was he following her? How had he known she was stranded?

"I was passing by on my way home," Rusty explained as he settled her in the truck, "and I saw you standing there, looking a little lost."

"Yes, well, Brad isn't too happy right now. Stranding me is the least of what he would like to do to me."

Rusty chuckled, and suddenly Brad's childish temper tantrum struck her as funny, too.

The two of them were laughing loudly when they arrived back at the inn. Sherry, uncomfortable now that Rusty had turned off the engine, glanced toward the inn with some trepidation. What was the protocol here? Should she kiss him good night as a thank you for being her knight in shining armor, or should she shake his hand, or just get out of the truck with a thank you and not touch him at all?

She wanted to touch him, though. That was the problem. She knew, instinctively, that if she offered to spend the night with him again, he wouldn't say no, but she also knew that would be the worst thing she could do right now.

She was too fragile emotionally, and another night with this man who haunted her dreams would drive her over the brink. So, without another thought, she opened the door and hopped down.

"Thank you for rescuing me again," she said before she closed the door and ran up the steps to go inside.

Rusty, watching her go, muttered, "By the moon." He put the truck in gear and headed home.

Sherry, leaning against the door, listened to the fading sounds of his truck and sobbed.

CHAPTER 17

a fter leaving Sherry in the restaurant, Brad drove around until he found a bar. Its rustic interior wasn't his usual type of place, but he needed something to slake his thirst, and this would fit the bill.

The place was occupied by a handful of tables scattered about the dirty floor, at which were seated some couples and groups of drinkers. Three rough-looking characters in plaid shirts were bellied up to the bar, and several couples and a few rowdy men in matching bowling shirts were drinking and talking.

The dark interior of the bar smelled of stale beer and sweat, staple odors for a place like this. Wrinkling his nose, Brad made his way toward the bartender. As he sat down, he gestured for the man's attention, ignoring the slurred comments from three men who sat nearby. Ordering his drink, he stared at the large moose head that occupied the place of honor on the back wall. Several other heads were mounted in various positions around the room.

"Where you from, mister?" asked a voice at his elbow.

Brad thanked the bartender who'd brought his drink and tried to ignore the men who were now sitting on either side of him and the one standing behind him, pressing close enough he could smell the man's cigarettes in their package.

Smelling them made him hunger for one, but he took another sip of his drink instead.

"What brings you here, mister?" asked one of the other men.

"You too good to talk to us?" asked the third. There was a threat in his voice. Brad looked down the bar, but the bartender ignored his plight.

"I'm just visiting your fine state," he said as he took another sip. He figured about ten more sips, and he could slip on out of here.

"Yeah, where you staying?"

"A place nearby."

"You one of them?" asked the first one who'd spoken.

"Them?" Brad asked, confused. He took another sip. Nine to go.

"The strange ones," said the second man. His breath was stale, and Brad tried hard not to gag. Another sip. Eight more to go.

"Strange ones?" he asked, then cursed himself. He hated that he was encouraging them, but they seemed to want to talk, and talking was better than robbing him. He didn't trust any of them as far as he could throw them. Another sip. Seven more to go.

"Yeah, some of the folk around here ain't quite right. You need to watch out. There are rumors."

Brad took another sip, then a second one. Five more to go.

The men warmed up to their tale and told Brad stories, but not the normal small-town kind of gossip he expected. More like the kind parents told children when they wanted them to behave, about wolves and other animals that were not just animals.

"You should probably stay out of the woods," the third one repeated for the fifth time, his voice slurring more now that his glass was empty.

Brad gulped down the rest of the drink and thanked the men for their stories. He hurried from the bar.

On the way back to his motel, Brad considered what those men had said. What if they weren't just rumors? What if there really was something weird going on in that town? What if that ranger was part of it? Wolves, huh?

CHAPTER 18

*R*usty, preparing for his nightly prowl, felt a need for speed tonight. He decided to do another perimeter run around the town at the end of the night, his fears for Sherry overcoming his common sense. He could call Sheriff Kasun and let him know he suspected something might happen with her ex-fiancé, but he selfishly wanted to be the one to watch out for her. And really, he had nothing concrete he could point to for the sheriff to get involved at this point.

Roaming the mountainsides and trails around the town, he found nothing out of the ordinary. Nearing the back of the inn, he once again stayed in the shadows. His wolf form sensing no unusual scents or sounds, he finally turned away.

As he roamed about on his patrol, Rusty caught a whiff of Brad's odor. He stopped, and lifting his nose to the air, he turned, trying to discern where it came from and how long ago, but the smell was too faint, disappearing on the wind. While it unsettled him, he couldn't go after the man simply for smelling bad, so he dismissed it.

A little while later, Rusty reached his stash of clothes and transformed back into his natural shape. His nakedness highlighted silver by the moon, he dressed quickly and returned to his home where he went to bed, falling into a deep, exhausted sleep.

~

SHERRY ROSE the next morning with a new attitude. She ate in the small dining room of the inn and walked outside. Just as she reached the gate, Brad met her. He wore a huge grin on his face, and groaning, she began to turn back around, but he grabbed her arm.

"How are you this morning, darling? Going anywhere special?"

"No," Sherry said, trying to shake off his grip. He didn't remove his hand, but instead increased the pressure of his hold. "Brad, stop it. You're hurting me."

As if on cue, Rusty drove up in his truck. Pulling over, he stepped in front of the two and motioned for Brad to let her go.

Brad laughed. Pulling out his phone, he turned and confronted Rusty.

"You might want to back off, ranger," he said, waving his phone like some kind of flag, "or I just might have to reveal your little secret."

Rusty looked at him with a wary expression while Sherry jumped to his defense.

"What are you talking about? You're the one with secrets!"

"Am I? Why don't you ask your lover here what he does at night?" Brad turned to Rusty with a smug look.

"What do you mean?" Sherry exploded. Grabbing Brad's arm, she spun him around to face her. "What are you up to? I told you already. It's over. We're over!"

Brad leaned closer to her. His voice lowered, and his eyes stared deeply into hers. "Baby, I love you, can't you see that?"

"You love me, and every other woman you can get your . . . hands on." Sherry glared back at him.

"I know. I'm not perfect." Brad looked humbled, ashamed even, as he begged her to reconsider her decision. "But I love you. I really do."

"Sometimes love is not enough, Brad." Sherry said.

"But it used to be all we needed." He reached out and touched the side of her face. Encouraged when Sherry didn't flinch or slap his hand away, he continued, "We are perfect for each other. We have plans," he whispered.

For just a moment, Sherry's heart wavered at the mention of their plans and the thought of the life full of love she'd always wanted. She could see in his eyes that he thought his ploy was working, but she knew it was just that—a ploy. He could never give her that love, that life.

"No," said Sherry, her tone cold. "There isn't room for me *and* all your secrets in our relationship."

"So it's secrets you don't like, is it?" Brad said, his voice hardening.

"Yes," Sherry agreed. She stepped away from him, closer to Rusty.

"At least I'm not a freak," Brad snarled.

"Don't be a jerk, Brad!" Sherry grew angrier by the minute.

"What if I told you your lover wasn't natural? What if I told you he was a werewolf? Would you still prefer him over me?" Brad clicked on his phone, and the video played.

Sherry watched, fascinated, as a beautiful russet-colored wolf changed into a man, naked and unmistakably sexy in the moonlight.

Unmistakably Rusty.

Sherry's eyes widened as her gaze went from the video to Rusty.

"What? What is that?" Sherry said, her expression confused, and then, "It was you. You're the wolf, and the angel, and the man all wrapped up in one package, aren't you?" Her voice came out in a strangled whisper, as if the truth was suddenly clear.

Rusty didn't deny it, but the look he tossed at Brad was murderous.

"This isn't how I wanted you to find out," he started to say. His eyes begged her to let him explain, but she backed away.

Brad, triumphant, restarted the video and said, "Yep, I'd say that wolf thing is a secret. Kind of a big secret, right, Sherry?"

"This changes nothing between us, Brad. I still want you to leave me alone. I want nothing more to do with you. Especially not now. I'm not sure what I ever saw in you, but I see you clearly now."

Rusty reached out for her, but she deftly avoided his hands, waving him away, too.

And with that, she turned to run down the sidewalk toward the garage.

"But Sherry, baby, you can't be serious. I'm not a freak at least!" Brad shouted to her receding back, but she ignored him, focused on the garage and the hope that her car was ready so she could get out of this place.

~

RUSTY, watching her go, wasn't sure whether he wanted to follow her or throttle her former boyfriend. He wasn't worried about Brad spreading rumors about him. Once he left town, the video would disappear and the memory of this place would be wiped from Brad's memory by the town's magical wards, but the damage to his relationship with Sherry was irreparable, and for that, he wanted to kill Brad.

Rusty, fists clenched at his sides and his face darkening with the promise of bodily harm, faced Brad, who had turned a lovely shade of white as if afraid and backed up a few steps.

Holding his hands up, Brad said, "Okay, man, don't rip my throat out. I don't want to be a werewolf."

Rusty, through gritted teeth, said, "I'm not a werewolf, you idiot. But I could rip your throat out and wouldn't regret it for an instant. If you don't leave town right now, I might just forget my oath to not harm humans."

Brad, realizing he'd finally crossed the line, quickly turned and ran to his car. He peeled out, and Rusty watched him speed down Main Street, barely stopping at intersections as he headed out of town.

Rusty slowly walked toward Joshua's. He had to explain. But he wasn't exactly sure how to do it. How did you tell the woman you had just met—and rescued from a situation that *you* caused—that she was meant to be with you? Oh, and by the way, you were a man who could shift into a wolf?

He frowned when he found Sherry in Joshua's office, sobbing in his friend's arms. The quiet man looked up when Rusty entered with eyes that begged for help. Strong emotions were hard for the man.

He'd usually left that up to Evelyn, who'd been a strong empath as well as being a shifter.

"Sherry," Rusty said quietly.

She looked at him and then quickly buried her face in Joshua's chest.

"Sherry," Rusty said again.

Finally, with a great sob that wracked her body into shivers, Sherry turned and faced him. Her eyes blazing, she spat out, "You lied to me."

"No," he said with calm certainty, "I didn't lie to you. I just didn't tell you the whole truth."

"You were the wolf that caused me to nearly die," she said.

"It was the storm that caused you to fall," he defended himself. Rusty took another step closer to her. "But, yes, I was the wolf you saw in the woods."

"You were the naked angel who saved me," she whispered.

"Sort of. I was naked, but I'm no angel."

Her gaze traveled up and down his body. "You were the man I made love to, or was that a lie, too?"

"No, that was not a lie." He stood as she watched him through tear-filled eyes, like she was trying to gauge the sincerity of his words.

"*Why* did you make love to me?" she asked, her tone beseeching him to explain.

"Because . . . because you are the one. You are my mate. You are my world." He paused, but pressed on. "That song . . . it was written for you."

"You wrote that song ages ago. How could it be about me?" Sherry's tears stopped flowing. She watched him with hungry eyes, and he knew he had to couch his words carefully or he would lose her forever.

"My kind love only once and forever. We wait lifetimes for a mate who will be our equal. And sometimes, sometimes the mate is not our kind. But that does not make the bond any less strong. You were sent to me by the moon goddess. I am yours, and you are mine. You were mine before I knew you." He spoke simply, sensing that her tumultuous emotions would not be able to accept the harsh truth of what loving someone like him would bring to her. Both the highs and the lows.

If she could accept him, accept *them*, he would gladly deal with any backlash when the time came.

Sherry looked at Joshua and said in a near whisper, "This is what it was like for you and Evelyn, wasn't it? This feeling of not being good enough, or of just not being *enough*, isn't it?"

Joshua nodded. "You are a child to one such as him, an infant, but you will grow old together. This I promise you."

Turning to Rusty, Joshua said, "If I can do anything to help you two, at any time, you only need ask."

Then, nodding to the two of them, he slapped Rusty on the shoulder.

Rusty nodded in gratitude and then turned to Sherry. Everything rested on her decision, after all.

Sherry, eyes bright with tears, turned back to Rusty and said simply, "I love you. I loved you the second you touched me. I don't know how I know that, but I believe you are my fate."

Rusty, hardly daring to believe her honesty, said, "You're sure?"

"Yes, my love." She moved toward Rusty, holding out her hand. "I'm sure. You are mine, and I am yours. Old wounds be damned. We will face what comes next together."

"Oh, Sherry, my darling. I cannot promise you our journey together will be easy, but I can promise you it will always be filled with love. Although our love might be . . . unique . . . it will never be normal or dull."

Sherry laughed a deep, throaty laugh that sent shivers down his spine. "Normalcy is highly overrated. Unique is much better when it comes to pleasing the heart."

Lowering his lips until they almost touched hers, he whispered, "Then get ready for some of the most heart-pleasing times of your life."

He leaned slightly away, taking the time to brush a hand across her cheek, sending shivers of need racing through her.

Sherry knew, glancing up into his soft brown eyes, that nothing could hold her heart more truly than the man whose desires turned him into a beast.

She pulled Rusty's face closer to hers, lips meeting his with all the confidence that comes from knowing, without a doubt, that you have met your equal.

WE HOPE you enjoyed this story in the Havenwood Falls series of novellas featuring a variety of supernatural creatures. Keep going for an excerpt of *Fate, Love & Loyalty* by E.J. Fechenda. The series is a collaborative effort by multiple authors.

Subscribe to our reader group and receive free stories and more!

IMMERSE YOURSELF IN the world of Havenwood Falls and stay up to date on news and announcements at www.HavenwoodFalls.com. Join our reader group, Havenwood Falls Book Club, on Facebook at https://www.facebook.com/groups/HavenwoodFallsBookClub/

ABOUT THE AUTHOR

Susan Burdorf is the author of several YA Contemporary novels as well as numerous short stories in a variety of anthologies. She is thrilled to be part of the shared world stories of Havenwood Falls and looks forward to many more adventures within its magical boundaries. A resident of Tennessee, she is often found hiking the trails on the hunt for waterfalls. Susan can be reached on her Facebook page at www.facebook.com/susanburdorfauthor and on Twitter at @sburdorf.

ACKNOWLEDGMENTS

A book is a collaborative effort even when written by a single author. In this case, *Old Wounds* is a work of collaborative teamwork of the highest degree, and I want to thank Kallie Ross Mathews for the loan of her character, Sheriff Kasun, and Kristie Cook for the loan of Michaela, the owner of Whisper Falls Inn, and also for the invitation to join the growing world of Havenwood Falls.

Thank you also to Regina Wamba of MaeIDesign for the amazing cover that brought Rusty to life; and to Liz Ferry of Per Se Editing for her work making this project so fantastic to view. If I have forgotten anyone, I apologize, but know how much your knowledge and expertise is appreciated by this humble author.

A Havenwood Falls New Adult Novella

Havenwood Falls

Fate, Love, & Loyalty

E.J. Fechenda

Fate, Love & Loyalty (A Havenwood Falls Novella) by E.J. Fechenda

Aster McCabe couldn't be happier with her job managing Coffee Haven and baking blueberry scones the whole town raves about, especially her sweet and sexy boyfriend Patrick. She loves her simple, small-town life in Havenwood Falls. At least, until her sister suddenly shows up with trouble not far behind.

The sisters' relationship has always been volatile, especially with the pressure of being the Alpha's daughters and the expectation to be perfect. Reeve never failed in that department, and Aster grew up in the shadows of her sister's success. But when Reeve left for college, Aster blossomed. So she's dealt a painful blow the moment her sister walks in the door and meets Patrick—a mountain lion's call to its mate couldn't be any more obvious. Neither can it be controlled or refused.

When an unstable Alpha from another den claims Reeve as his mate, Aster, bitter over the recent betrayal, practically draws the guy a map to Reeve's location, unknowingly putting her entire family and den in danger. Aster must figure out how to right her wrong and save her family. But loyalty and love are further tested when a stranger appears with the potential to forever change Aster's fate.

FATE, LOVE & LOYALTY

AN EXCERPT

*T*he bell above the front door chimed, and Aster McCabe looked up from the espresso machine, anticipating her boyfriend since she'd been counting down the minutes all morning. They were going away to celebrate their six-month anniversary with a long overdue trip to her family's cabin located in a remote area in the mountains. There they'd be able to shift and run and hunt together, away from the watchful eyes of the community. With Patrick being new to the den and new to Havenwood Falls, there were some who viewed his attachment to Aster as more of a strategic political move. Being the alpha's daughter placed Aster and anyone she became involved with under more scrutiny—a fact that she hated. She always felt she was being held to a higher standard than the other members of their den, and her perfect sister, Reeve, had raised the standards even higher. At the thought of her sister, Aster scowled. The last time Reeve had been home was for Christmas, right before Patrick had shown up in town, and they'd fought constantly.

Instead of Patrick, Aster's boss, Willow Fairchild, walked in cradling her swollen belly—the reason why she'd been showing up later and later for work. A gust of wind followed her in, carrying the sweet fragrance from catalpa trees that were in full bloom. The town square across the street was home to several of these towering trees, which had more fluffy white blossoms than leaves.

"How are you feeling?" Aster asked, deftly steaming milk without even looking at the machine.

"Good. Tired. The baby kicked up a storm last night." Willow eased into a chair at one of the few empty tables near the front counter.

"I can cancel my weekend away if you're not up to running the shop," Aster offered as she handed a latte to a waiting customer.

"No, no. You and Patrick have been planning this. I'll be fine, and Paisley is able to work some extra hours." Willow dismissed Aster with a wave of her hand before resting it back on top of her baby bump. With her white-blonde hair and pixie features, Willow looked barely old enough to be pregnant. While her fae heritage gifted her with a youthful appearance, she was really six years older than Aster. After Aster graduated from college in December, Willow promoted her to manager—a timely decision, since Willow found out a month later that she was pregnant.

Shadows under Willow's eyes, more noticeable because of her porcelain skin, made Aster worry. What if she left and something bad happened? Willow had become more like the sister she wanted, and Aster suddenly felt guilty about leaving. Was it selfish of her to go? She attempted to shrug off the negative thoughts, but it was too late. Willow had already received them. It was hard to hide anything from her boss, one of Havenwood Falls' most powerful empaths. She sensed emotions from miles away.

"Stop it, Aster," Willow said. "You worry too much about what other people think. You need to get out of here and let loose—it will do you some good."

Aster smiled and smoothed her apron, wiping at a clump of flour from a batch of her blueberry scones that won Best of Havenwood Falls two years in a row. Streaks of white powder stood out against the black fabric. "I know."

Willow's command was easier said than done. Having grown up in Reeve's shadow, Aster had years of feeling insecure holding her back.

Reeve had moved to Denver and had been gone for more than six years, but the comparisons never stopped. Reeve was high school class valedictorian, she was Miss Teen Havenwood Falls, and she practically walked on water. Guys of all species salivated in her wake. Back then, Aster had been an awkward teenager, and puberty hadn't been kind. All knobby knees and elbows with carrot-orange hair that stuck out in a riot of uncontrollable curls, she was a far cry from beautiful Reeve. She was even envious that her sister was able to leave Havenwood Falls to move to the city, where she lived a glamorous life. Of course, the Court of the Sun and the Moon, the governing body for supes in town, made an exception for her and lifted the spell that usually made other supes and humans forget their time spent in Havenwood Falls.

"You're doing it again." Willow's voice broke through Aster's thoughts. "Have you heard from Reeve?"

"Not lately. She's probably busy planning some extravagant event for some celebrity." Aster turned around to open the oven door. Heat blasted her skin, and the sweet aroma of blueberries and cinnamon assaulted her nostrils. She grabbed an oven mitt and pulled out a tray of golden-brown scones, setting them on the marble counter to cool. She loved the old-fashioned counter and that she didn't have to worry about using a cooling rack or hot pad.

"Aster, you have carved out your own life here and landed an awesome job with the coolest boss ever. Oh, and you have a hot piece of man meat. Who knows, soon you could be sporting one of these." Willow patted her baby bump dramatically, making Aster laugh.

"No! Hell no! I'm not ready for that." Aster shook her head in denial, her ponytail swishing along her back with the movement. Her once carrot-orange hair had darkened to a light auburn, and the longer she grew it, the more the curls relaxed. These days she had grown to appreciate her locks, but had to keep them pulled back. No one appreciated hair in their scones. While she disagreed with Willow on babies, she did agree with her about having an awesome job.

Aster surveyed the shop, taking a moment to admire all of her hard work over the past year. Paintings from local artists hung on the red brick walls, adding color to the space. At Aster's suggestion, Willow had added flower boxes to the large front picture window, and the wildflowers that bloomed were a cheerful greeting to anyone walking by outside. Several hanging plants inside, along with Willow's crystal collection, added a quirky vibe. Overall, the effect was relaxing and inviting. Combined with the good coffee and food, Coffee Haven was a favorite among locals and visitors.

"Well, it's going to happen one of these days, because you're a catch. Why do you think eighty-five percent of our customers are male?" Willow winked, because at that moment Patrick walked in the door. "And all of them are hot for you. Feelings . . . I pick up on these things, you know," she said and tapped her temple.

"Who's hot for you, besides me?" Patrick said with a growl. He stalked across the shop and around the counter, pulling Aster into his arms. She sank into his warmth and breathed in his musk. He rubbed his cheeks against her hair, an instinctual way of marking her with his scent. She tilted her head up, and he slanted his mouth over hers, sending the message to any male in the coffee shop that she was taken. This sent a shiver through her, though she never would have admitted the whole display of male dominance turned her on. Of course, Willow picked up on it and started to giggle. Aster flipped her off behind Patrick's back, which made Willow laugh even harder.

"You ready to go, babe?" Patrick asked when they separated.

"Yes," she responded breathlessly. "My bag is upstairs."

One of the perks of being manager of the coffee shop was the apartment upstairs, which Willow rented to her at a reduced rate, since having a mountain lion shifter living upstairs was added security. Aster untied her apron and tossed it in the hamper under the sink.

Just as they were preparing to leave, the bell above the door chimed. Aster turned to see who was coming in and froze in place. *What the hell was Reeve doing here?* There her sister stood, wearing simple jeans and a black T-shirt, but still managing to showcase every curve. Her hair looked like she had just had it professionally styled; auburn waves framed her heart-shaped face. While Aster was momentarily stunned, Patrick was not, and she watched in disbelief as he prowled toward Reeve.

"Patrick?" Aster called, and she reached for his arm, but he shrugged her off. "Patrick!" she said louder, and he looked back at her briefly with a dazed look in his eyes.

He blinked once, slowly, before focusing on Reeve again. Aster stared in disbelief as she noticed Reeve's dreamy expression and how her sister tracked Patrick's every move. Then she realized what was happening, and her stomach dropped to her toes. She'd seen this before, when their brother Braden met his wife, Kaitlyn.

"Oh, shit," Willow said from behind the counter, and Aster looked at her. "I'm so sorry, honey." Her bright blue eyes shone with sympathy.

Willow's confirmation hit Aster like a punch in the gut, and she bent over as if in physical pain. She couldn't breathe and couldn't process what was happening. Reeve wasn't even supposed to be there in the first place.

"Unbelievable!" she screamed. "You always get everything. Why?"

She couldn't bear to look at them anymore as they scented each other and began touching every inch of exposed skin, oblivious to anyone else around them. With a sob, Aster stormed out through the back of the shop. As soon as she was in the alley behind Coffee Haven, she stripped off her clothes, shifted into her cat form, and took off for the woods on the outskirts of town. She didn't care that running through town as a mountain lion was frowned upon or that there would be consequences. All she cared about was running far away from her sister before she did something stupid, like gouge her eyes out with her claws . . . or kill her.

For Reeve McCabe, meeting her true mate couldn't have come at a worst time. She wanted to fight it, but was powerless against the attraction. She felt inexplicably drawn to the handsome stranger in the coffee shop, and he became her only focus. She smelled her sister's scent all over him, and it made her want to pounce on him to claim him right then and there. Aster. The only reason she stopped by the coffee shop to begin with. She broke away from her mate's gaze when her sister cried out and winced when she saw the hurt on Aster's flushed face, her red cheeks stained with tears. When Aster took off, Reeve ran after her.

She called out for Aster to come back, but by the time she reached the alley, Aster was gone, her clothes a discarded heap on the pavement. Reeve started to call her cat forward so she could pursue her sister, but her cat had nothing but mating on her mind and refused to cooperate. She was unable to leave her mate. She didn't even know his name or where he came from, but that didn't matter. Now that they'd crossed paths, she knew she'd never stray far from his side.

She had come to tell Aster she was home for an indefinite amount of time. Life had gone sideways in Denver, and she needed the security, the protection, of the den and her family. Trouble had followed Reeve lately, and sadness weighed heavy on her heart when she realized the source of her sister's anguish. Her mate was Aster's boyfriend. Shit. Without even meaning to, she had once again caused her sister pain. With a sigh, Reeve picked up her sister's clothes and folded them. She brought them inside and left them in a neat stack on top of a cardboard box before returning to her mate.

"I feel just as shitty, too. Aster doesn't deserve this. She's a good person. I've seen you in the pictures she has in her apartment. You're Reeve?" her mate asked in a deep voice that echoed within her soul. He brushed a tear off of her cheek before his hands came to rest on her hips, and she felt the strength they possessed. His eyes were a warm brown, framed with thick lashes. His light brown hair was long on top and tousled. A straight nose brought her attention to his full lips.

"Yes," she replied and stepped closer so their bodies were a breath apart. "And you are?" His heart pounded a strong, steady beat, and she was shocked to discover her heartbeat had already aligned with his.

"Patrick O'Shea." A hand left her hip and ghosted up her side, lightly brushing against her right breast before cupping her cheek. She leaned into his touch and purred. All thoughts of anything except Patrick disappeared when he touched her. She knew they had an audience in the coffee shop, but she didn't care. The instinct to fully mate with Patrick clouded her brain. "Please tell me you have your own place, because I'm staying with my parents."

Patrick smiled, his canines already grown longer, and his eyes flashed golden. "I do. Let's go."

They quickly left Coffee Haven, a boatload of pheromones following them out the door.

Patrick lived in Havenwood Village, an apartment complex located a block away from downtown Main Street. At the speed they ran, they reached his apartment within minutes. He opened the front door, and that's as far as they got. Patrick pressed her up against the wall and lowered his head to capture her lips. She tilted to meet him and growled in appreciation when they connected. His lips were soft, but the kiss was hard with urgency. She parted her mouth and welcomed his tongue while burying her hands in his thick hair and tugging on it, encouraging him to deepen the kiss. Reeve moved her hips forward, and as if in sync, Patrick did too. His arousal pressed against her belly, and she broke off the kiss.

"I can't believe this is really happening," she panted.

"Me either," Patrick said between kisses that he traced from the corner of her mouth and along her neck. She tilted her head back, giving him more access. He brushed her long auburn hair behind her shoulder and gently bit down on at the juncture of her neck and shoulder. His canines just barely broke the skin. The act of dominance triggered waves of lust.

"Wait, I don't even know you, and what about Aster?" she asked, trying to retain a grip on reality and not be consumed by her emotions. Reeve's voice shook as she struggled to form the words.

Patrick groaned, but raised his head to meet her gaze with glowing eyes, his irises darker slits, echoing her struggle for control as his cat called to hers. "Trust me, Aster needs her space, and honestly, I don't think I can stop. We will get to know each other—we have our entire lives to learn everything there is to know and so much more."

He kissed her again, and Reeve allowed her cat closer to the surface. She shifted enough to allow her hands to transform into paws tipped with sharp claws, and she shredded Patrick's shirt. He growled with approval, his eyes flashing golden again right before he sliced her shirt open with an equally sharp set of claws. Soon their shredded clothes lay in a pile on the floor, and they stood naked before each other without any shyness.

Reeve admired her mate, running a hand down his muscular chest and stomach. He had a few scars on his side—faint claw marks that had faded to white—which she guessed were from an old injury. Leaning forward, she gently licked the scars, then placed a soft kiss on his skin. His scent filled her nose, and her whole body pulsed with a powerful wave of arousal. She gasped and stood up straight, almost dizzy with need. Patrick looked her over appreciatively, and her skin flushed under his gaze. His nostrils flared, and his eyes glowed amber right before he spun Reeve around so she faced the wall.

"I don't have the patience to be gentle or slow, but I promise the next time . . ." He ran his nose along her neck and cupped her breasts from behind. She arched her back and pressed into his hands. With every touch, she felt her hold on reality slipping, her conscience suppressed by the call to mate. Every nerve in her body hummed with promise and came alive with each caress.

She whimpered as she stopped resisting. "Take me. I'm yours."

The moment he entered her, Reeve knew there would never be another man for her. Their souls merged, and she felt his need as acutely as her own. His hard, muscular body pressed her against the wall, and she pushed back against him, causing him to drive deeper.

"Oh my God," Reeve cried out, and her knees threatened to go soft.

Patrick brushed her hair aside and bit down on her neck. This time his teeth pierced her skin, completing his claim on her. An overwhelming sense of peace and pleasure consumed her as she felt her blood surging into his mouth. With a final thrust and grunt, Patrick stilled and rode out her orgasm while licking the bite mark clean. They stayed pressed against each other, their pulses pounding, for a few moments, catching their breaths. Reeve slowly turned around to face her mate. His hair stuck out in all directions, and his cheeks were flushed from exertion. Reeve wrapped her arms around his neck and stood on her tiptoes, pulling him to her for a kiss. Now that the initial itch had been scratched, the urgency had waned, but after a few strokes of her tongue, Patrick was ready again.

This time they faced each other. She raised a leg and hooked it over his hip, and he slid inside. They moved in sync, creating a rhythm that quickly rose to a crescendo. Patrick lifted her up, so she wrapped her legs around him. From this angle, she was at the right height to stake her claim. She licked the spot on his neck first, and the vein pulsed underneath her tongue. Her canines dropped, and she struck, drawing his blood into her mouth. The iron-rich warmth bubbled up, and she drank deeply until Patrick released with a muffled groan. Then she retracted her teeth and licked the wound. She was his, and he was hers. The mating bond was officially complete, and there was no going back.

After they collapsed in Patrick's bed, sated and drowsy, the guilt set in.

"I don't regret finding you, my mate," Patrick said as they lay in his dark bedroom. "But I just hate that Aster is hurt. I do care for her, but now, you're all I can see."

"I know. I tried to resist, but the mating call . . . I've never experienced anything so powerful before. Poor Aster." Reeve sighed and rolled over onto her side to face Patrick. He moved so she could settle against him with his arm tucked in behind her, holding her close. "It's not like I planned this. Trust me, I have enough complications in my life, and I just added another reason for my sister to hate me forever."

PURCHASE *Fate, Love & Loyalty* at your favorite book retailer.

www.ingramcontent.com/pod-product-compliance
Lightning Source LLC
Chambersburg PA
CBHW052009170626

46808CB00007B/2853